Mar/Apr '02,
Easter Bunny!

THE GIRL
WITHOUT ANYONE

Kelli Deeth

THE GIRL
WITHOUT ANYONE

Harper*Flamingo*Canada

www.harpercanada.com

HarperCollins books may be purchased for
educational, business, or sales promotional
use. For information please write:
Special Markets Department,
HarperCollins Canada,
55 Avenue Road, Suite 2900,
Toronto, Ontario, Canada M5R 3L2

First edition

Canadian Cataloguing in Publication Data

Deeth, Kelli
The girl without anyone

ISBN 0-00-225500-6

I. Title.

PS8557.E326G57 2001   c813'.6
C2001-930137-5
PR9199.3.D43G57 2001

01 02 03 04 HC 4 3 2 1

Printed and bound in the United States
Set in Bembo

—for my family

ACKNOWLEDGMENTS

I WOULD like to thank my mother, Mary-Jean Deeth, for her unfailing support and encouragement over the years. In addition, I'm grateful to Carolyn Swayze, Karen Hanson and Iris Tupholme.

NIAGARA FALLS

WE WERE sharing a room. I'd only seen hotel rooms in movies, once in a book about a New York secretary. The bedspreads were a mash of flowers, the furniture appeared weightless, and the room was cooler and darker than outside. My father and Selena dropped their duffle bags in front of the dresser and stretched out on their bed, as if a tide had beached them. Selena, who was twenty-seven and wore large eyeglasses, the frames of which matched her dirty-blonde hair, laughed in a low French accent, tickled him in the side. Then, lying on top of him, she compared her slim hand to my father's wide one.

"Big baby," she said.

"You're the big baby," my father said.

She put her hands on his large ears, kissed his thick hair.

I turned on the television, flipped channels. The commercials were American and everyone looked too

friendly and out of date. Selena and my father didn't
notice when I quietly opened the balcony door, sniffed
the air that smelled different from the air in the suburbs
near Lake Ontario where I lived with my mother and
brother. When I turned, my father's hand was resting on
the back of her shorts, as if gently and thoroughly he was
checking the temperature.

I stepped outside and sat in the white plastic lawn
chair.

Selena was in the bath, singing a song in French, when
my father joined me outside in just his Adidas shorts. I'd
been bitten twice on the arm and once on the bum, and
I'd taken out the braid Selena had put in my hair.

"Enjoying the Falls?" he said, sitting in the white lawn
chair with his legs up, curling his long toes over the
edge; the ugliness of his toes drew my eyes.

I said, "I can't see them," just as he said, "Braid looked
cute."

"I looked like an ant."

"Listen to Selena."

"Can we go for a walk?"

"Why?"

"Just to walk."

"I don't feel like it."

I had the sudden wish that Selena would be dead when
we went back inside the room. My father would be
momentarily sad, then he would see that it was for the
best, and we would ride in the car with our hair blowing in the wind.

He flicked his cigarette over the railing of the balcony.
"One day down."

Later, I had to change into the T-shirt I slept in. I locked the bathroom door because my father had a habit of not knocking. Selena's and my father's deodorant sticks stood side by side like miniature silos. I breathed in the steam, which contained Selena's perfume, Impulse. In the mirror, I looked like someone else, a person no one knew. When I opened the door, my father was just clicking off the lamp, lifting up the blanket, and I couldn't tell whether he was wearing pyjamas or not. He put his free arm around Selena.

"Night."

"Night."

I stretched out on the bed, on the cool sheets. Selena giggled in a high, hollow voice, and there were wet noises, my father's teasing growl. I held my breath for a moment, just to hold it. The giggling wouldn't stop. I had lists of prayers, but selected one, that my house would still be there when I got back. To help myself fall asleep, I pictured drapes opening and closing, something I'd learned in my health class.

The next night, after a day of shopping and eating, I told my father I would stop breathing if I did not see the Falls, but he didn't want to go without Selena. "You have hurt my poor feet enough today," she said, switching channels. Her hair was in a terry-cloth turban because she'd just come out of another bath.

My father took the keys and winked at her. "Don't let in any strangers."

Outside, walking fast along a sidewalk, my father wore

a new, stiff baseball cap, a buttoned-up jacket, and from the side I could barely see his eyes. I held an ice cream in one hand and wrapped my other arm around me because I was shivering.

"We'll save the Falls for tomorrow," he said.

We drifted into an empty park with a slide and monkey bars, where my father started doing chin-ups, grunting, hissing his breath out evenly.

"I hope you're exercising properly," he said. "This is how you live longer, you know."

"Selena kissed someone," I said. "Some man."

"You saw Selena kiss someone?"

"When you were in the bathroom at the restaurant."

"No."

"He was wearing a tie," I said. "And his face was sunburnt and he gave me ten dollars."

I revealed the ten dollars my mother had given me.

"She did, did she?"

"On the lips," I said. "Then he got into a car and Selena told me not to tell."

"Told you not to tell, eh?"

I nodded because I had run out of steam. There was nothing left of the lie. My father told me to come closer to him, and as I did, it was like approaching a king: he would judge me, and good or evil could occur. He put his arm around my neck and I believed I had won the day, but then he squeezed my head into a headlock, held it.

"You're lying," he said. "Who taught you how to lie like that?"

"I'm not."

"You've been listening to your mother." He added that Selena was a saint. "I love her."

And those were the words: my whole body felt slapped. He held me in the headlock for a moment and I wanted to give up resistance, but I struggled.

"I'm going home," I said into his sleeve. My father let me go, and I started walking and he walked behind me, leisurely.

"How are you going to get home without me?"

"Walk or hitchhike."

"You think so?"

"I'm going to."

"You think you could do that, huh?"

"I'm going right now." I stopped walking.

In the dark, cool air, my father studied me as if I were a new product, something tough and remarkable.

"Well, goodbye, then," he said, walking ahead, his shoes making sounds in the mud. He called back for me to send him a postcard when I got there and to watch out for coyotes. "They like little kids." Then he turned around and his red jacket grew smaller and smaller in the darkness, like a plane's tail light.

I would go home. I would be the girl without anyone who found a way to survive. I stepped across the field, the hems of my jeans getting wet.

I walked along a sidewalk, passed a church, then came to an intersection, busy with cars and filled with the smell of exhaust.

When the fluorescent walk signal appeared, I crossed and kept going straight, hoping I would recognize something. The wind blew through my clothes as I passed a donut shop, almost familiar, then a gas station I couldn't remember having seen. At the corner of the gas station stood a phone booth, like a beacon, and I stood inside it, shut the door, which was covered in fingerprints. I found a quarter in the change from the ice cream and I put it into the slot, let it click. I dialed my number at home, but the operator came on and said in a harsh, nasal voice that I had to insert more quarters because it was long distance. I imagined my mother at home, playing solitaire at the kitchen table, with a cigarette in the ashtray, a glass of red wine, always red, half empty.

I hung up, opened the phone booth doors, squinted in the direction of the hotel, but I saw nothing, only the smallest cars, a strip of yellow. I continued along the road, counting my steps. A woman with heavy mascara slowed to gaze at me with puzzled eyes. I was truly on my own. My father would pick Selena up in his arms and they would clap their hands. The tips of my fingers grew hot, and so did my head, and the land around me expanded, everything, stores, fences, growing farther away, but larger; I could not keep a grip on what was around me. On my fifty-third step, I heard a car behind me. My father's green Rabbit pulled onto the road shoulder ahead of me, puttering. He shut off the engine. Selena's head poked above the headrest, a dim blonde cap in the dark. I did not know what he would do. I walked past the car, warm and lit up inside, my back stiff.

Selena got out of the car. "You're not going anywhere."

I kept walking, though it was harder to put my feet down. I heard a car door slam, then feet on the gravel.

I kept my back straight, and my father caught me around the neck.

"Where do you think you're going?" he said. He smelled of smoke and I breathed it in.

The next night, my father wrote postcards, even though he would be back in two days. To braid my hair again, Selena sat me down on the bed in front of her, her long legs stretching out on either side of me, the skin as smooth as a peeled peach. When she had tied my hair up, she rubbed my shoulders, dug her thumbs in, massaging me.

"You're like wood," she said. "You must miss your mother."

"No."

My father put down the postcards and came over to pull on my braid. "You should wear it like this all the time. It's not so scruffy."

Because he was talking to me, I didn't argue.

Selena let me dip my finger into her container of flavoured lip gloss. I rubbed my lips together and tasted cherries, distantly. I wondered if my dad tasted it when he kissed Selena.

"We're going out for dinner," she said, standing up. It was a sudden idea.

"Let's just take it easy," my father said. He pulled oranges and apples, bread and peanut butter, out of a grocery bag—three cans of Coke.

She put her arms around his neck: when she was that close to him, her body took on the look of a wet cloth.

Something you press onto yourself. My father rested his
hands on her hips, and I could tell that she was having an
effect on him because he looked at her in a way that he
never looked at anyone else, a way that suggested she
was providing him with warmth. His shoulders relaxed.
He smiled, dazed.

"What's another night out?" he said. I wanted to jump
in the air, to knock him down with a hug.

After glancing out at the darkness, my father put his
coat on, a hat that said Niagara Falls. Selena wanted to
wear a sweater, but he said no, she had to wear the jacket
that was identical to his, and she did. Dressed the same
as Selena, my father looked truly happy, like a small boy,
someone who had been given the prize.

When I started to buckle up my denim sandals, my
father said, "Where do you think you're going?"

"Out."

"Girls who lie don't go out."

"But I'm hungry."

He threw me an orange. Then he patted Selena's bum.
"If you go outside you won't be able to get back in." He
dangled the key.

Then he came and kissed me goodbye on the forehead, a prickly kiss. Selena blew me one from the
door—that was her style. Then he guided her out of the
hotel room, a hand on her shoulder, and I had the
impression that one of them was blind.

When I could no longer hear their footsteps outside,
I sat down on the bed, breathed deeply. Perhaps this was
how Selena felt in one of her endless baths—calm, as if

she could never be bothered, annoyed. My father and Selena's bed was neatly made, without a wrinkle. In my duffle bag, I had a needle and thread because it was my mother's bag, and she carried a needle and thread everywhere. I unzipped the front compartment, pulled the needle out of the thread, tested its sharpness against my finger, letting it stab. I pulled back the blankets on my father's bed, poked the needle through the sheet on Selena's side, poked it back through so that it was sticking up. I pulled the thin blankets over it.

Careful to leave the door open, I went out on the cool balcony, the cement freezing my feet. They were down below walking through the parking lot, and Selena walked slightly ahead of my father.

I changed into my T-shirt, lay under the blankets, and I did fall asleep, listening to doors opening and closing, keys, cars in the parking lot, gently revving. What woke me up was Selena singing "Morning Train" in English. Then they were both speaking French, my father managing with what little he knew. And he used his sexy voice, the one that turned his face red. I controlled my breathing carefully as they took off their clothes, brushed their teeth; the Impulse bottle hissed. Before they got into bed, my father leaned over me, and this tenderness caused me to realize that I had done something wrong, made a horrible mistake.

The hotel room was quiet. With my eyes open, I tried to name every object I spotted in French, but then I heard a noise, a female noise of pain. The light switched on and I closed my eyes.

"It's a needle," my father said.

I sat up in bed and rubbed one eye. "What happened?"

"Did you put this here?"

"What?"

"You know what." He was pulling on jeans over his tight blue underwear, and Selena lay on her stomach, her hand at the very top of her thigh. I could not see any blood, but I could not tell for sure because my father had turned only one light on.

"It's in the bone," she said.

My father threw her the terry-cloth robe, then he pulled back my blanket, exposing my bare legs. "Get dressed."

When I had finished dressing, I sat at the table while he held her up so she could put her feet in sandals. At night, Selena's nose was large.

My father put her clothes in a grocery bag.

We shuffled outside where everything seemed vast, echoing. In the car, Selena had to lie down on the back seat, so I sat in the front, my body electric.

"I didn't put it there," I said.

"Shut your mouth," my father said.

"I didn't do it." I added that the cleaning woman had probably done it, by accident, and my father said that cleaning women weren't that stupid.

"You miss your daddy," Selena said. "You and your mother will enjoy this. Enjoy seeing me hurt."

The hospital came into view, lights glowing harshly, and I thought of what would happen to me if anyone found out. My body grew hot, so hot that I wanted to roll down the window.

"Everybody just shut up," my father said.

When we arrived, he helped her limp to the emergency room, and because it was late, she was seen right away, by a doctor in a green cap. My father followed them down a bare hallway with the grocery bag.

In the waiting room, I stared at an old man who crossed his arms. I stared even though I knew he knew I was staring. I pretended that I couldn't help it, that I was not aware of it myself, my perverse ailment. I paraded past him with some quarters, bought a Mars bar from a vending machine; I would give it to my father.

I was smoothing the wrapper, making it warm, when they walked Selena into the waiting room.

"Did they get it out?" I said.

My father didn't look at me, but placed a gentle hand on Selena's shoulder. She got the gentlest of his touches.

"Harold," Selena said. "I want out of this circus." She took his hand and gripped it severely, the way a mother would hold a child's hand. "This cannot go on."

"Circus?"

"You are the circus leader and this girl is the main act." She let go of his hand.

"Listen, sweetie," my father said softly, as if talking to a small bird.

"Call me a cab."

"No."

"Harold," Selena said. "You know better than to argue with me." And I wished he did know, that he knew he was a fool.

My father obediently, like someone tamer and smaller than himself, went to the front desk, where the nurse put down a sandwich to give him a heavy black phone. I had never seen him give up before, and I wanted to deliver the Mars bar, have him taste it, feel content. He asked the nurse the number, then dialed it; as he listened to it ring, he gazed at Selena's profile, his mouth small. I sniffed the wrapper.

Then he walked her outside, and I watched them from behind the emergency room doors. He was pulling on Selena's hand, then he kissed it, then he held her other hand and gave it hard kisses that would leave red marks. She tried to pull her hands away, but my father kept gripping them, pulling them towards himself. Finally, he let go.

I kissed the glass, lightly.

I watched him rest his hand on her shoulder until the cab pulled up.

He set her in the back seat, and in it, her form was as straight as a cigarette, as firm; I wondered if she would be cold without her coat, which was still hanging in the hotel room closet. My father watched the blue and white car pull away and I did, too, watching her head grow smaller and smaller in the dark. I wondered if he had given her enough money.

My father started for the car without looking back at me, and I opened the doors and followed him to it. The Rabbit was as square as an ice cube, and inside, the vinyl interior smelled of Selena's Impulse.

"Did she leave you?"

"No."

When I looked at him, his lips pressed together so

hard, his mouth had the shape of a slightly hooked beak.

"I want to see the Falls."

"You happy with yourself?" He turned the key in the ignition.

"I want to see them."

We drove, but I couldn't tell where we were going, if we were returning to the hotel, or just driving, the way my father sometimes liked to. The streets all looked the same to me, the street lights, trees, everything. Maybe he would take me away and I would never return. I pressed my hands so hard against my legs, they drained of blood like straws. There was a current of something strong and terrible connecting my father and me in the front seat, something that held us together. I sliced open the Mars bar with my teeth, took the tiniest nibble of chocolate, then set it in my lap; I would make it last all night.

My father drove silently, his hands easy on the wheel. I knew I might never get to see the Falls, that I was close to seeing them, but might never actually stand at the rail and see what I was supposed to see.

And that was the way it was with my father: he could disappoint you. The first night I had ever stayed in his apartment, when Selena had been visiting Montreal, I had lain on the firm mattress of the spare bedroom and listened to him snore. But I was a girl who could never get close enough, who could never show enough love, and I had pushed my blankets back, crept into his bedroom. I had gently, carefully, lain down beside him; I had held my breath as I touched his back.

He had woken up, and as I had pretended to sleep, to be unconscious, he had carried me back into the spare bedroom; he had kissed me on the forehead.

I took my eyes off the road to look at him.

"I've decided I'm not your daughter." It was the meanest thing I had ever said, the most strangely pleasing.

"You can't force someone," he said.

I studied him, his skin that hung, his large eyes. I took another nibble of the Mars bar, chewed and swallowed, watching the white road lines disappear.

FLORIDA

MY MOTHER drove leaning forward, as if on the look-out for small animals, and I saw several semi-detached houses that could have been his. In William's territory, we inched so slowly, it was like space travel.

She pulled into the driveway of a green semi, checked her eyes in the rear-view, lowering her glasses to her nose. Then, leaving the car running, she got out, climbed up the stairs, her body expressing resigned determination. After banging on the aluminum door, she examined one sandal, lit a cigarette, and inhaled calmly, flicking the ash over the side of the porch. Finally, I saw Sharon peek through the sheers of the front window and squint at our car. Her expression was militant, hurt.

I unrolled my window. "Let's go," I said, because I wanted to go before we saw Alec, Sharon and William's son who I had found tadpoles with when his father had lived with us.

My mother, who had not seen Sharon, slashed a dramatic line across her mouth, meaning quiet.

Then Sharon opened the front door, black hair hanging over one eye. She wore a pink jogging suit with clean white runners.

"Off of my property," she said.

"I would like to apologize," my mother said.

"Off," Sharon said, closing the green door in a swift motion, as if trying to keep out a demon.

"Listen, lady," my mother said, as she pulled on the locked handle. In the front window, brown drapes slowly met each other.

My mother stamped her cigarette out right onto the cement porch, grinding it in with the toe of her sandal. Wearing white slacks and a white blouse, my mother was slimmer, bold.

She brought the smell of cold into the car, lit up another cigarette, and kept it in her mouth as she backed out.

"Where was William?" I said.

She took the cigarette out of her mouth, set it in the ashtray.

"Where does she get off?" my mother said, her voice thin, as though she spoke at a higher altitude.

"Where was he?"

"Out."

She drove steadily past the intersection where she should have turned, and each time she braked, the car jerked. I had the impression that if we met a cement wall, my mother would drive into it.

"He's not coming back," I said.

"That man would die for me," she said. "Make no mistake."

She pulled over onto the gravel, near a field. Still holding the steering wheel, she rested her cheek on it, and the flatness of her mouth suggested a hunger I could never have fathomed.

"He has not an inch of desire for that woman," my mother said. I wanted to stroke her back, but I kept my hands tightly clasped.

She raised her head. "He's coming back," she said.

After checking traffic, my mother started the engine, pulled a U-turn, and we drove in the direction of our house, which would be empty. I rolled down the window, though it was chilly, and tried to keep my eyes open in the wind. I did not know what made my mother happy, what would ever make her happy.

At home, I pushed back my blanket in the quiet darkness. My mother had gone to bed soon after we'd arrived, because she had to get up at six to make it to work. She was an executive secretary. I shuffled to the phone, my feet cold on the floor, the floor right above my brother's room, so I made myself light. I dialed the number I had memorized from the phone book, let it ring. Finally, William answered, his voice alert and puzzled, and I hung up.

In the park, I met Alec, who had a leaf of black hair. I had not seen him since William had left. What I noticed was that he had not changed in height, but he behaved as if he were taller; he held his spine in a way that suggested he possessed the key to a castle where the gates were closed. Before, he had followed me around.

We took turns climbing the metal steps of the slide. After I had taken one of my turns, I stopped him while he was still at the bottom of the steps.

"Can we go to your house?" I said.

"I'm not allowed to talk to you."

"I'll give you a dollar," I said.

Alec jumped off the step. "Two."

From my sock, I pulled out the money. Alec took it, untied his shoe, and shoved it to the toe.

To get there, we cut through the ravine, walked along a sidewalk for a mile, then crossed a bridge. Alec stopped to buy a root beer with the two dollars, sucked it up through a straw while we walked. When we got there, his house was cool, tidy, with a large mint sofa, an oak dining set with cushions strung to the seats. The kitchen was immaculate, the tiles white and shining. A bowl of chips sat on the counter, an offering. In his room, Alec lay on his side on his captain's bed, and I looked out the back window onto their square backyard, its pruned maple tree. Sharon, painting the back fence, kneeled in white shorts, and William, wearing only jean shorts, dragged a net through the pool.

"I'm going swimming," I said.

"You just want to see him."

"Who?"

"My dad."

"I don't even like him."

I went out quietly, passing through the large kitchen

with the portrait of a fish on the wall. Finally, I was on
the bright patio behind him. I reached up to tap his
shoulder and he turned, startled, his face burned red.
Without a shirt, his ribs showed.

"Leah," he said. "What brings you here?"

"Water."

Sharon dropped the lid on the paint can, carried the
can to the patio.

"Did your mum send you?" she said, her skin shining
with moisturizer.

"No."

"Are you sure?"

I nodded.

Sharon squinted at me; I must have been reflecting
harsh light. "I hope you do not tell lies." Then she went
into the house, carrying the paintbrush.

William went into the shed and I followed him there.
Inside, there was the smell of dust, iron, William's sweat.
He hung the net on a hook. He was tall, his body was
flat, as if it had been pressed, and his arms were freckled.
In the dark, I could still see that his cheeks were red, and
his chin was pointy, delicate. My mother had told me his
toes were webbed, and never to look at them; I had
come to believe that all British men had webbed toes. I
sat on the bench.

"Can I go swimming?"

William's face was smaller than I remembered. His
eyes were small too, as if he were just waking up, and I
tried to see them as my mother did.

"You want to go swimming?"

"Yeah."

"You should be out enjoying Lake Ontario," he said, but I found the beach in our part of town too cold, crowded.

"I like pools."

"It's getting late," he said. "Aren't you hungry?"

"No." Then I changed my mind. "Yes."

I told him another man loved my mother, a man named Gord whose house we had visited to eat ham sandwiches. My mother had told me that Gord wasn't too quick on the uptake, but I told William we were moving in with him, and that he had bought me a jean jacket.

William smiled, showing small, yellowed teeth. "I'm exceedingly happy for you."

"I have to go because he's picking me up." I stood.

"So long, Leah."

Wearing the tennis outfit she had once played tennis in, my mother sat in a lawn chair, her hair wet, reading the newspaper.

I sat in the driver's seat of the car, which was parked at the top of the driveway. I had unrolled the window, and I was trying to imagine that I was on an endless road, but I could not help feeling bothered and distracted by my mother sitting next to the hood, her white, thick legs in the sun. She was smoking slowly but anxiously, taking deep noisy puffs. The seat of the car was prickling and hot, like sand.

"Can we move to Florida?"

"Why do you want to move to Florida?"

"So I can get away."

"I'm not moving to Florida," my mother said.

"I'm going," I said. "And I'll never come back." Then I told my mother I would beg for money, that it would be better than living with her.

"And what did I ever do to you?"

"You had me."

"You love your mother."

"I don't."

"And how about if I didn't love you?" my mother said, steadily. But when I opened my eyes, her face was crumpled and the newspaper lay flat in her lap.

"I would say good," I said. "I would say thank you very much."

My mother rose, her mouth flat.

"Say you love me."

Before I could answer, she went into the house, letting the screen door snap shut behind her.

My mother did not speak to me. We watched television on the same couch. When she fell asleep in the living room, I took a blanket from the linen closet and put it over her.

He liked ice cream. When he had lived with us, my mother had served it to him nightly, vanilla, strawberry, walnut.

One night that week, my mother didn't change out of her work clothes, and she brushed her hair as if she were punishing it.

"Let's go," she said, following me into my bedroom.

"Where?"

"Ice cream."

I wore her heeled sandals, but with socks, to hide my toenails; it was difficult to walk to the car, but I kept my shoulders back. We drove through the heat to the ice cream parlour. Before we went in, my mother insisted that I smell her armpit.

"I forgot the damn deodorant."

I smelled it. "Fine," I said.

Then my mother took a deep breath, and she shivered as she let it out. "Hither we go to battle."

William was already sitting in the parlour with Sharon and Alec. They each had a bowl of ice cream sprinkled with nuts. Both William and Alec wore short-sleeved plaid shirts, something else that proved they were British. Sharon wore a sundress with thin straps, and she had dyed her hair burgundy.

"Ruth," William said, stretching his neck. "Thirsty for some ice cream, are you?"

"Thirsty, thirsty," my mother said. "Small world," she added tightly. She gave me her black purse and told me to order two banana splits.

"I'm rewarding my daughter for mowing the grass. Isn't this place a little out of your way?" She spoke to William, glancing like a thief at Sharon. From the counter, I watched Sharon spoon her ice cream as though she had an endless supply. Alec bit his, chewed it. He had a spot of chocolate on his chin.

"William has to have his ice cream, Ruth," Sharon said.

"He does."

"I just can't keep him away."

"Certainly can't."

"Thinking of staying?"

"Yes," my mother said. "My daughter desires it."

My mother found a table against the wall and breathed urgently until I sat down. Her breathing was shallow, almost a pant, and she spooned the dessert frantically. I glanced at them. I smiled at Alec, but he popped a cherry into his mouth. Sharon had both William and her precious son Alec because her hair was cut short at the ear, her eyelids were mauve, her lips moist. She knew how to keep them—and this was the kind of woman who held a family together, who got what she wanted and did not lose.

"Eat up," my mother whispered.

"I am."

William touched Sharon's hand. When their bowls were empty, he stretched in the chair, patted his stomach.

"She's following you, Dad," Alec said, so loudly that even the boy at the counter turned.

"We came for ice cream," I said across the aisle.

"Sure you did. Yeah, right."

"Mind your mouth," William said to Alec.

Sharon rose, zipped her black purse, brushed Alec's bangs out of his eyes.

"Lovely to see you, Ruth," William said, standing.

My mother sucked a piece of banana, swallowed hurriedly. "On this summa evening," she said.

Sharon, from the door, said goodbye to my mother grandly, as if my mother were a child. My mother waved her five fingers.

When they had left, she let the ice cream melt in her dish.

★

She came home from work exhausted, carrying a dress coat over her arm, letting the long belt drag. She held on to her briefcase with three fingers. It was Friday night, and my mother would begin it by drinking two glasses of red wine in the corduroy easy chair. She would not be drunk, only moodily weary, and she would lie on the couch.

But tonight, my mother sipped a glass of milk. She leaned against the counter, cooling down. Her clothes smelled burnt.

"I want you to clean the bathroom," my mother said. "We're having a visitor."

"Who?"

"Guess," she said, smiling. She opened the fridge, removed a jar of pickles.

"Dad," I said, because he was the most remote.

My mother frowned, as if this reply saddened her. Then she placed her claws around the lid of the pickle jar, bent over, pressed her teeth together. "Guess again," she said, strained.

"Who?"

The jar popped open and she straightened. She opened the utility drawer, found a fork, and stabbed a pickle. She sucked on the end before biting. My mother loved sour tastes.

"William," she said, impatiently. She turned her eyes from the pickle and met mine. Her eyes were uncertain, gauging the enemy.

"Hang up my coat," my mother said. She finished the pickle. "Then I want the bathroom spic and span."

I hung up her coat in the hall closet, straightening the belt, then closed the closet door. For the bathroom, I used an abrasive cleaner on the sink and tub, the perimeter of the floor.

In her room, my mother removed her glasses, splashed water on her face, then looked closely at her eyes. I had seen thick, almost smudged black eyeliner only on my mother—the other women I saw drew thin, neat lines, and I attributed her inability to do this to her lack of vision. Without her glasses, she saw only colours.

I sat on the bed before her mirror, brushing my hair. To ensure effectiveness, she had already plugged in the curling iron, one bought from the salon we went to.

"Why's he coming?"

"Because," my mother said, "he never wanted to go back to her, Leah." She moved like a worm to get out of her green velour dress. "He only did it for Alec."

She peeled off her nylons, smiled at me. "I see you blushing," she said. "Get used to it. It's the human body." She found black lace underwear in her top drawer. From the closet, she yanked black slacks. I picked out her top, a red, orange, and yellow striped V-neck. My mother looked decent, though her hair was still flat.

Curling her hair, she kept a cigarette going.

She said that all her euchre friends had told her to forget William and move on. But she never had. "I knew."

She hurried to Mac's Milk and returned with cold meat, which she arranged on a plate. She spooned mustard into a bowl, relish into another. In the middle, she placed an unsliced loaf of bread, something she had never bought before. Two wine glasses and two dinner plates. She stretched Saran Wrap over the meat. "Do we have any candles?" she said. "Go check the bottom drawer of the bookcase."

I found an old Christmas candle that smelled of pungent wood.

"That'll have to do," my mother said, smelling it.

She set it in a dish, then rested a package of matches, from a basket on top of the fridge, beside the candle.

"Now, I don't want you getting your fingers into this," she said. She dug into her purse. She straightened a five-dollar bill, gave it to me. "Go get fish and chips at the take-out place. When you come home, come in the back door." Then she said, "Damn." She fished perfume out of her purse, sprayed her wrists, then rubbed the residual on her neck and her top. She sprayed my hair.

"Now you're as lovely as Mummy."

Cleaned and perfumed, she sat on the couch and read the newspaper. Every so often, she touched her hair.

"When's he coming?" I said.

"Soon," my mother said, without looking up, pursing her lips.

I stood outside and stared at our driveway, our yard. It was the quietest house on a street where one father played basketball with his son, where our neighbour mowed his lawn, and where the brothers across the street played hockey in the driveway with a tennis ball. It not only sounded quiet, it appeared quiet; my mother was always on her last drop of energy, tired, so our two front bay windows were bordered only with burly shrubs. There was no front garden. Still, this summer, in a cement tub at the side of the house, she had managed to make flowers grow, red geraniums. As I walked my bike down the driveway, I strained my neck to feel the warm wind on my face; summer was ending.

I folded the five dollars into my pocket, climbed onto my red five-speed, and started riding. I glanced at our house as I passed it, and it looked like a grave.

I rode uphill to the fish and chips take-out restaurant, and I could smell it before I could see it. Fish and chips was the highest of treats, the servers could never give me enough. The French fries never lasted, and I always feared that I might never have them again.

I leaned my bike against the front window, stood in line behind a man wearing a red T-shirt. His black hair was short and reminded me of Gord's, the man who had not been quick enough on the uptake. His back was wide, his arms hairy. I bet that he had a swimming pool.

I scanned the menu above the kitchen. In the pictures, the food was glossy, large. The man in the red T-shirt placed his order and stood to the side. A woman with a blonde wig said, "Yes, dear?"

I asked for change, gave her a dollar, and received quarters in return.

As I opened the door, bells clattered. I walked my bike across the parking lot, then started riding. I rode down a long hill and through the ravine. Then I bumped along a stretch of sidewalk that led me to the bridge. I rode past a plaza into a residential area where the houses were three stories, and the lawns large, displaying ornaments. I stopped when I got to the green semi-detached house. The drapes were closed, but there was a car in the driveway. I got off my bike, left it at the end of the driveway by a large pinkish rock.

I banged on the screen door. While I waited, I ran my finger down the cool aluminum frame, and my fingertip turned black.

The heavy green winter door opened slowly, and Sharon's hair was the first thing I saw, no longer burgundy, but shining black. She wore olive eyeshadow up to her eyebrows and wouldn't come out from behind the door.

"Yes?" she said.

"I have to give Alec something," I said.

Her black eyelashes must have grown heavy. Pressing her lips together, she studied my clothing, my bare legs. "One moment," she said, and closed the door completely.

While I waited, I pressed my foot against the screen door. Alec opened the heavy inside door, already in his pyjamas, toothpaste at the corner of his mouth. I told him to come outside.

"No," he said. "My feet will get cold."

"I have to tell you something."

"What?"

"William's coming back to my mom," I said. "Tonight."

"Liar."

"He is."

Alec opened up the screen door, stood on the cold cement. Then he slapped me so that my cheek burned.

"Liar," he said.

A tooth felt loose, and I tasted something warm and salty.

Alec opened the screen door, stepped inside the house. There was a light on behind him. "I'm telling," he said, and he stared at me, his black eyebrows arched. Sharon passed behind him into the kitchen.

Holding my cheek, I walked down the driveway to my bike. I climbed on. It had gotten suddenly colder because the sun was down. Keeping my tongue on my tooth, I rode my bike along the empty street. It was the most expensive area of town. When it was first built, my mother and I used to drive through it, picking out houses. I chose the ones with the most levels and my mother chose the ones with the largest lawns. She wanted everything large. At the stop sign, I had a sudden urge to get home quickly. Something was going to happen to my mother, she was in danger.

At that moment, she would be sitting on the couch, her legs crossed, waiting.

I rode, my legs tiring, giving out.

PET THE SPIDER

I HELPED Loretta rake the lawn, which was covered in soggy orange maple leaves. Loretta's Aunt Phyllis sat through the sliding glass doors watching *Magnum P.I.*, as she did every afternoon. She had an illness that left her unable to move, and Loretta said she had come from Scotland to die.

"Can we feed her?" I said

"Feed who?"

"Your aunt."

"You mean, go within ten feet of her?" Loretta said, biting her lip, raking furiously, because her father, Mr. Beatty, was meticulous about his lawn.

"I'll feed her, you can watch."

"Whatever gives you a thrill."

Inside, Aunt Phyllis sat in her wheelchair, gazing out onto the backyard, her hair combed down over her eyes and ears.

"And we could fix her hair," I said. I rolled the

wheelchair into the kitchen, which Mrs. Beatty had recently painted red and white.

"Do I look like a beauty technician?" Loretta said.

"You going to a dance, Auntie?"

Aunt Phyllis groaned, and I smoothed her hair.

"Just for herself," I said.

"Aren't you a ball of fun," Loretta said.

I took a carton of strawberry ice cream out of Loretta's jammed freezer. I thought Aunt Phyllis would like strawberry ice cream because it suggested femininity and delicacy.

I sat in the chair before her and spooned it into her mouth. I dabbed at the sides of her mouth with a serviette.

"She understands," I said.

"Two plus two," Loretta said. "Come on, Auntie, hold up your fingers."

They lay still in her lap. But I thought she was trying.

"You can tell when she makes noise," I said. "I think."

"Auntie just likes to be heard. You should hear her go to the bathroom."

Aunt Phyllis's eyes moved slowly to Loretta, and I could tell Loretta had gone too far, been cruel. Aunt Phyllis's eyes were almost closed.

Loretta put her arm around Aunt Phyllis's neck, kissed her cheek repeatedly. Aunt Phyllis panted.

"She doesn't like that," I said.

"I love you, Auntie," Loretta said, squeezing harder. "I'm sorry, Auntie." Loretta's voice was high, hyper.

"You're making it worse," I said.

Loretta was laughing, trying to catch her breath. "Oh, Auntie, you crack me up."

I spooned in more ice cream, trying to show Aunt Phyllis that I knew she was uncomfortable and probably hated Loretta. "She knows what's going on," I said.

Loretta caught her breath, put her hands gently on the sides of Aunt Phyllis's head.

"Auntie, would you tell me if you could understand?"

I watched Aunt Phyllis's fingers. Instead, Aunt Phyllis closed her mouth.

"Watch," I said. "Is your husband dead or alive?" I stared at the fingers—moving a finger up meant yes. But they remained still on her thigh. Mrs. Beatty said Aunt Phyllis was losing the ability to move even those.

"She's decided it's sleepytime." Loretta kissed the top of Aunt Phyllis's head, rolled her into the living room. Loretta lifted one arm and I lifted the other, then we pulled her onto the couch and tried to sit her up straight. I turned her head towards the television and placed a pillow behind her neck.

Loretta changed the channel to a soap opera everyone in the family assumed Aunt Phyllis was interested in. Mrs. Beatty had even told me that Aunt Phyllis had a crush on a character, a young gardener.

While Loretta went into the kitchen to pour us pop and to fill a bowl with chips, I entered Aunt Phyllis's empty bedroom. It smelled of floral freshener, stale air, and a decaying sweetness, even though the window was open. The wallpaper and curtains were mauve, and the two dressers were white with fancy gold drawer handles, the kind on a girl's dresser. On her bed lay a mauve quilt.

I opened the closet and saw Aunt Phyllis's clothes, a brown blazer, dresses with belts, clothes belonging to her when she could speak and walk. It was an Aunt Phyllis I could barely imagine, one who could enter a room of her own accord. I closed the closet and went to the dresser. On a lace doily, the kind that Mrs. Beatty fashioned herself, sat a black-and-white picture of a man and a woman. They were the same height, and wore long wool coats. The man had his hand on the small of her back and the woman, her hair pulled back, a black hat on her head, was smiling with an expression of gratitude.

I went back into the living room and sat beside Aunt Phyllis. I did something daring, something I didn't even think about first. I placed my hand on her shoulder, to tell her I cared. But it startled her, and she made a snorting sound of fear and alarm. I took my hand away quickly.

The wind was coming down from the north, but it had not yet snowed, even though it looked every day as if it would. It was the time of year when my mouth tightened on the walk to school because the cold, biting and stinging, seeped through my scarf.

Sitting in my grade eight classroom near the end of the day, looking out the window, I tried to imagine, as I often did since Aunt Phyllis had come from Scotland, what it would be like to be unable to move. But the noise of the classroom made concentration difficult.

After school, I wanted to go to Loretta's so I could feed Aunt Phyllis. I wanted to have some sort of conversation with her. I wanted to know how she felt about death, if she was scared to die.

"Why can't we go to your house?" Loretta said. "I'd like to watch your brother jam. Maybe he could teach me how to play."

"Tomorrow," I said. My brother and Dan, his friend, who were both in grade eleven, had skipped school and gone to Toronto for the afternoon, and wouldn't be jamming.

Inside, I saw Aunt Phyllis's head first, the scalp visible. Her gaze was focused on *Magnum P.I.* Mrs. Beatty, who took care of her during the day, was pulling knee-highs onto Aunt Phyllis's legs.

"Keep her while I go to the IGA," Mrs. Beatty said.

"I'm not a babysitter," Loretta said.

Mrs. Beatty slipped her bare feet into sandals, though it was autumn.

"Spare me your tongue."

She slammed the door.

I rested my hands on the handles of the wheelchair and smelled old skin, a salty, horrid smell. "She needs a bath," I said, firmly.

"There are some things I don't do," Loretta said. "I don't go near naked bodies."

"But how would you feel?"

"I would have a vodka and orange juice," Loretta said. "Nothing wrong with a little dirt."

"She needs a bath," I said. I did not look forward to seeing Aunt Phyllis without clothes on, but there was a part of me that had to know, had to know what her body would look like, be like—I had to go through with it.

Loretta turned off the television with her toes.

"If I help you, we watch your brother jam for three days in a row. Deal?"

"Why do you want to see him so bad?"

"I have my romantic future to consider," Loretta said.

"Fine." It suddenly occurred to me that I should ask Aunt Phyllis if she wanted a bath, but something told me it was safer to assume that she did—that when it involved dirt and a body, you had the right to assume. I rolled her into the bathroom, onto the pink bath mat, and after that, I avoided her eyes; they were bright, glaring.

I ran warm water, not too hot, and I squeezed in bubble bath.

"A bubble bath," I said, smiling at Aunt Phyllis, trying to appear light-hearted, friendly. Because giving a bath was an act of compassion. But Aunt Phyllis's face hung, her mouth tugged downward, as if she were trying to figure something out, trying to listen. I had the sudden sensation that Aunt Phyllis could read my mind, that she knew that it was wrong. I should ask her first. Aunt Phyllis would think hateful things about me—that I was cruel, that I knew better, but didn't care.

I tried to pretend that it was just a bath, just a bubble bath. Aunt Phyllis would want to be clean, and I had been compassionate enough to notice.

I took one arm and Loretta took the other of the heavy pink sweater, and when we pulled it off, Aunt Phyllis's hair rose in static electricity. I kept my eyes on Loretta's face, which was scrunched up.

Her bra was lace and her breasts sagged in it like water balloons. There was an added intensity to Aunt Phyllis's eyes. She hated me. She would kill me if she could.

I was not sure I could carry on, and felt like vomiting.

"Flabby," Loretta said.

"She understands," I said.

"You know I love you, Auntie," Loretta said, pulling Aunt Phyllis's head to her own breasts. "I'm just teasing you because you have a bit of flab."

"One day this will happen to you," I said.

Loretta frowned, bit her red lipstick.

"You going to take it off?"

"We have to."

"Go ahead," Loretta said.

"I'm thinking."

"She's getting cold."

"Why can't you?"

"Who wanted to give her a bath?"

The word *bath* helped me remember our mission, and that's what it was, a mission. My eyes fell on Aunt Phyllis's pink arms, the diamond on her ring finger. Someone had loved her.

"Fine," I said. I leaned forward, got my arms behind Aunt Phyllis's back, and unclipped the bra. As I pulled it off, gently, Aunt Phyllis hummed in a high voice, an angry whine. That she hated me could not be mistaken.

"Do the rest," Loretta said. "And hurry before the water gets cold. Would you want to take a bath in cold water?"

I could not possibly turn back. It was my fault Aunt Phyllis was half undressed, and I would have to go through with it, get it over with. I grabbed Aunt Phyllis's burgundy slacks around the waist, and pulled, the underwear with them. I turned my mind into a complete blank, a whiteness that allowed for no feeling. My eyes saw things I refused to absorb. Helpless things, a bright pink body, thin legs, grotesque helplessness. I would punish myself for what I had no right to see.

We each peeled down a knee-high.

Loretta spoke in a kind, strained voice. "All right, honey, just take a deep breath while we lower you in."

My throat was closed. I simply performed my duty. I lifted Aunt Phyllis under one arm, under one leg, using the muscles in my back to hold her in a standing position. We moved her towards the tub, sat her on the rim. We slipped her legs over, then lowered her into the tub. Suds floated flat in the water.

Loretta soaped her. "You're going to smell so pretty," she said.

Aunt Phyllis was sitting in the water, getting soaped, and I was responsible. Loretta soaped her legs, her breasts, her bum, then quickly and brutally in the spot I could not look at. Aunt Phyllis was dying and couldn't move, and there was nothing I could do.

I kissed Aunt Phyllis on the back of the head. "Don't worry."

Aunt Phyllis began to cough in the night, Loretta said, and Mr. or Mrs. Beatty, or Loretta, had to get up and shake her to stop her from choking on her own saliva. Mr. and Mrs. Beatty said Aunt Phyllis was waiting to die.

But I didn't want to give up. One weekend, I slept over at Loretta's house. At dinnertime, Mr. and Mrs.

Beatty, Loretta, Aunt Phyllis, and I sat at the round table. Everyone but Aunt Phyllis ate scalloped potatoes, green beans, and pork chops. Mr. Beatty wanted Aunt Phyllis at the table so that she wouldn't feel left out.

Mr. and Mrs. Beatty talked about the fast-food chicken restaurant they had recently bought. Apparently, the cook kept showing up drunk and couldn't hit the toilet when he peed. Mrs. Beatty said they should never have bought the place, and Mr. Beatty said, "That's enough."

"Do you wish you could eat a pork chop?" Loretta said to Aunt Phyllis, whose eyes appeared to be closed. The slits widened.

"Leave her alone," Mr. Beatty said. "She's bad enough off without you waving pork chops in her face."

"I was just asking her if she missed them," Loretta said, her body tensing.

"She'll enjoy her applesauce later," Mrs. Beatty said.

"I wasn't saying she wouldn't," Loretta said.

"I don't think we should have her eat with us anyway, Tom," Mrs. Beatty said.

He put down his fork and knife and rolled her away.

After dinner, when Mr. Beatty had gone to the chicken restaurant, Mrs. Beatty sat with her arm tightly around Aunt Phyllis on the couch, and every once in a while, she would give her a kiss. Sometimes Loretta would get up and give her one.

"She'll die at home, at least," Mrs. Beatty said, pulling Aunt Phyllis close to her.

"Then God can take her to the bathroom," Loretta said, changing the channel with the converter. "Right

Auntie?" she said, but her tone suggested that Aunt Phyllis couldn't have understood what she had said.

I studied Aunt Phyllis, wanting to say something kind. "Her hair looks nice today," I said.

"It should," Mrs. Beatty said. "It took me all morning to get her head under the tap."

I wanted to say something more to her, to show her that I knew she did not want to die.

When the movie was over, Mrs. Beatty said, "Help me put her to bed." She got up stiffly, holding her back.

"Not now," Loretta said. "We'll do it later."

"Be quiet with the chair," she said.

For a while, we sat and watched music videos, colours flashing, but we could barely hear the television because the sound was so low.

"I think she wants to go to bed now," I said.

"No," she said. "Aunt Phyllis wants to party."

Loretta and I looked for a second at her closed eyes, and then Loretta said, "Whatever. All I see on t.v. are skinny chicks in tight clothes anyway."

The noise in Aunt Phyllis's throat started when we lifted her. I accidentally elbowed her in the side, and she made a high-pitched yelp. Then we had her awkwardly in the chair, one hip higher than the other, and she was huffing as if we'd attacked her. Mrs. Beatty banged on the wall, the sign to be quiet.

"Give me a break," Loretta said, under her breath. "Thanks, Auntie."

Loretta wheeled the chair and I walked in front, clearing boots and Loretta's textbooks from the path. Once we had her rolled into the bedroom with the door shut behind us, we turned on the light. The corner of the mauve quilt had already been turned down.

Loretta wheeled the chair around the far side of the bed, where there was a narrow space between the bed and the wall. They put her to sleep on that side so she would be closer to the radio, which was set on a shelf beside the bed, along with the china dolls that Loretta had brought in from her room when she had heard that Aunt Phyllis was coming from Scotland.

We each took an arm and lifted her, kicked the wheel-chair out from under her with our feet. We struggled to keep her up, and she made the vicious sound a dog a might make, a low, violent sound, and she was still fight-ing for breath.

Then there was a knock on the front screen door and Mr. Beatty's voice. "Would someone open the damn door?"

Loretta, who was always afraid of making her father angry, said, "Take her for a minute." I leaned against the wall and settled Aunt Phyllis on my leg. Her weight was manageable this way, but she was still a pressing force, and she couldn't hold her head straight. It fell back in my face, and all I could smell was her white hair.

"Just wait a minute," I said kindly.

Then I felt it, hot liquid spreading down and out across my leg, all over my thigh, down to my knee.

Loretta came back in. "Loser," she said about her father. Then she took Aunt Phyllis's other arm and we lifted her, pushed and pulled and shoved her onto the bed, which creaked. She didn't make sounds.

I didn't look down at my soaked thigh, and Loretta

did not see it. She noticed the urine when we pulled down Aunt Phyllis's green track pants, but she only held her breath. We both knew that we should have wiped her down, but neither of us mentioned it. We pulled her top efficiently off, and let her lie there with nothing on while we took her sleeveless nightgown out of the top drawer and unfolded it. Then we pulled it roughly over her head and bent her arms any way we had to in order to get them through the sleeve holes.

With the nightgown on, she lay stiffly, her breathing a little calmer. My thigh was sticky and warm, and the stench of urine was rising from my jeans.

I had to get a good look at her face, to see whether she knew what she had done to me, and to see whether she had done it on purpose to make me feel bad, to make me know that she knew exactly what was going on and had the whole time, to let me know that she wanted me to leave her alone. When I looked at her flat eyes, they expressed vast loathing, and I was not spared.

Loretta and I went to sleep in her double bed, which was really a pull-out couch, one she could fold up during the day. Loretta soon began snoring, loud, grinding snores. I couldn't sleep because all I could smell on my hands was Aunt Phyllis's skin. I left the room quietly and stood at Loretta's kitchen window, which looked onto the neighbour's kitchen window. Inside two panes of glass, a spider waved its leg.

I sat on the vinyl kitchen chair and pretended to be paralyzed. It took all my concentration to imagine, to feel that I could not move anything, even if I had to. I breathed deeply, kept every muscle still, until I was paralyzed. Anyone can do whatever they want to me, I thought, push and pull me. I can't move.

I wanted to move. I stood at the window where winter would be coming, winter that would fill every crack and hole. But it wasn't winter yet: somehow that meant I still had time. It wasn't over for me, and I shivered at the thought, a shiver in my chest from somewhere deep, permanent, felt only when it wanted to be. In the window, the spider was in the same place, but balled up, as spiders almost always were, and I petted it through the glass.

FIFTEEN ALMOST

MY MOTHER and William sat in the living room, as they did every weeknight, and read separate portions of the newspaper. My mother drank a hot Irish cream coffee that William had brewed, and her lips tightened for the heat. William sipped a red wine, his eyes drooping at the print, his face red. In the evenings, you could smell his sweat, but my mother told me that in some countries, nobody cared how you smelled. She added that William would die for each and every one of us. I imagined his death by sword.

Downstairs, my brother, Matthew, played the bongo drums that William had brought back from a business trip. Matthew's friend, Dan, whose hair stuck out over his ears, leaned against the couch, playing the bass guitar. Neither of them looked at me. I sat against the wall, writing math answers on a piece of paper.

When they took a break, I asked Dan if he had brought his motorcycle, though I had walked past it.

"How else would I get here?" he said, his foot tapping the carpet.

"Can I go for a ride?" I said.

Dan struck three loud chords. "Got your motorcycle licence?"

"I mean, can you take me for a ride?"

Matthew did a drum roll on the bongos. "Leah, leave us alone."

"Yeah, I'll take you for a ride."

Amplified chords drowned out whatever I might have said.

"Hold on tight," my mother said, standing in the front hall with her arms crossed.

"Daniel looks like a take-charge man," William offered.

Once Dan had the helmet on, I could not see his face. It was hidden behind a black visor. He gave me a white one that was too large, and I had to hold it in place.

Up to the stop sign, Dan drove at a normal speed, but once he turned the corner, he sped up, and my neck was thrown back. I wrapped my arms all the way around his waist, and when he slowed down, I kept them there.

When he dropped me off at the end of the driveway, I could not see his eyes.

"Thanks," I said. I touched his hand, which was cold, and remained perfectly still.

"See ya," Dan said, revving.

He would see me again.

Before bed, I did what I always did: kissed my

mother's cheek, covered in thin, dark down. It was like kissing something weaker than myself, something I couldn't protect from harm. William was soothing his back by lying on the Indian carpet, the wineglass propped on his chest, empty, his thin legs crossed. He would not expect a good-night kiss, or even a word, because he never got either.

In his basement room, Matthew was with an Italian girl he liked. Dan and I were sitting on the couch in the rec room, and he was blowing smoke rings towards the black light they had stolen for their band. Though there was a long space between us, we were sharing the same wool blanket with blue and black checks, and I thought this meant that we were joined. That was what I thought love was, a joining. And once I was joined, the person I knew as myself would neatly and finally vanish—I would no longer feel longing.

"You like playing bass?" I said.

"Why else would I?" he said, without turning his head to me.

The Italian girl let out a high-pitched squeal, a thrilled, startled laugh.

"I'm taking all the blanket," I said.

"You talk a lot."

"Most people like talking."

"How old are you?" he said.

"Fifteen," I said. "Almost."

He took his cigarette pack out of his shirt pocket and threw it to me. Inside it was a lighter that I used to light one of the cigarettes. I let the cigarette burn in my fingers, trying to decide what I could give him in return, trying to figure out exactly what he wanted.

"You can have the blanket," I said.

Staring at the television, he said, "You can have it, too."

"Thanks." Then I added, "I think I'm going to smoke all the time."

"Dumb," he said. And then I knew he was protective of me.

Matthew opened his door, shut it behind him, and came out with a sheet wrapped around him, one shoulder visible.

"Got a butt?" he said to Dan.

"She's got them."

I hurriedly gave the pack to him. After he had lit his cigarette, he laughed. "Having fun underneath the blanket there, Rat?" Rat was Dan's nickname.

"I don't think so," Dan said.

"Sure," Matthew said. As he opened his door, I saw the girl with a blanket pulled up to her chin.

Before I could say anything, Dan was up off the couch.

"Butts please."

"You're going?"

"Some of us have better things to do."

I walked behind him up the stairs, and he didn't say any of the things I was expecting him to say: stop following me, why are you coming upstairs?

I leaned against the wall as he put on his shoes.

"Tell your brother to get his own goddamned

smokes," he said. And he opened the door with a hard push, not looking back at me to say goodbye.

My brother and I drove my mother and William to the airport, because they were catching a plane to West Palm Beach, to talk, my mother said, about adult things, privately. The whole drive to the airport, I stared at the back of my mother's head. The skull was so frail. There was nothing protecting it. My mother could experience a sudden blow, the worst pain, her head smashed to little bits on a strange road. William would leave.

He bought everyone lemon Danishes while we waited at the airport, two hours early, at his insistence.

I held my mother's hand.

"My fingers are longer," I said.

"Yes, they are." My mother opened her mouth wide for the Danish. "You're the woman of the house now. That means keeping things in order." She chewed, swallowed. "Do you think you can do that?"

"Yup."

My mother patted my hand. "You're becoming a woman."

They had to leave.

My brother sprouted tears when he hugged my mother. He told her not to worry about anything, that he would take care of me, and that he would always be ready to take care of her. William hugged Matthew. When he looked at me, I crossed my arms.

I hugged my mother, and her flesh seeped into my own.

"Bye, my lovey," my mother said.

"Bye."

I waved to William, whose mouth was a straight pink line.

Matthew and I drove along the 401, and the only sound was Matthew chewing a Danish, the last in the box. He ate with his mouth open. Normally, I would follow my habit of pretending I was alone, and he would follow his habit of pretending he was alone.

"Dan coming over?" I said.

"You want to sit under the blanket with him again, eh, little Leah?" He made moist, appalling kissing sounds.

"I just asked," I said.

At home, I had the impression that the house leaked. There was something weak about our house; the outside always made its way in.

"I'm the boss now," Matthew said, getting out of the car. "You want to do anything, you ask me."

"I'm not asking anything."

It had gotten suddenly colder, and the wind was stronger, pushing at my ear.

"Then you pay the price."

Inside, I kicked off my shoes and went immediately to my mother's bedroom. I got under the covers, breathed in the smell of her pillow. I could even smell William, the faint smell of a body after sleep. Closing my eyes, I wrapped their thin blue electric blanket around me.

★

Matthew and Dan smoked a joint through the kitchen window. Matthew blew rings. "I bet she likes it up the bum."

Dan imitated the sound of a squeal.

I grabbed the Windex from below the sink.

"Who?"

"A pig," Dan said.

"Get out of here," Matthew said.

I sprayed the mirror in the front hall. Wiping, I heard the clatter of Loretta's bicycle wheels, then the rustle of a grocery bag.

Loretta appeared at the door wearing blue eyeshadow, which gave her eyes the shape of wings.

"Ha," I said, which was how we said hello.

"Ha," Loretta said. She gave me a significant look, raising the IGA bag. She had been able to get the booze, the Old Grand Dad, kept in her parents' liquor cabinet.

Before we did anything, I led us into the bathroom. I put on frosted pink lipstick.

In my room, we drank Old Grand Dad in mugs and ate chocolate icing out of the tin with our fingers.

"Are they going to play?" Loretta said, lying back on my bed.

"They play every day."

Loretta emptied her mug. "I think we should join the party."

I emptied mine.

We strolled into the kitchen.

Dan, wearing a white T-shirt imprinted with a Mack truck, rolled another joint at the kitchen table, his thick fingers performing a delicate task. Matthew dabbed mustard onto their bologna sandwiches. When he turned around, he told me to wash that crap off my face.

Loretta said, "You're just jealous because you wish you could wear it."

"Who asked you, bird nose?"

Loretta grabbed the hair on the back of his head. "Who you calling bird nose?"

"Bird nose." Matthew took her hand and held it behind her back. "Bird nose." He laughed. Then he pushed her away.

Loretta was gasping.

"Smell my breath," she said to me, glancing at Matthew. "Can you smell anything?"

"Ooh. The little kids have been into the al-co-hol."

Dan sparked the joint and offered it to me. His hands shook, and I took it as a sign of deference. Only nervous people shook.

Matthew grabbed my wrist.

"Drop it."

"No." I stared at him, attempting to convey a deadly seriousness. My eyes were my best weapons.

"One puff," he said. "That's it."

I inhaled as deeply as I could. Then I breathed it in again, let it out, breathed it in again. I passed it to Loretta, who blew smoke out without inhaling.

Dan told her not to waste it.

My mouth grew numb. Feeling this, I wished fiercely that I had hugged William goodbye.

Matthew took three short puffs in a row.

The whisky must have made Loretta bold because she

began to dance with Matthew. She draped onto his back, wriggled against it.

Though I'd only had three puffs, Dan was small and far away.

"Your eyes are red," Dan said to me. "Holy. Are your eyes ever red."

I felt myself slowly beginning to smile, and my brother told me to stop smiling.

Loretta would not let go of Matthew's arms. "When you teach me the bongos," she said. "When you teach me the bongos."

"You're not bongo material," Matthew said. He grabbed her breast and squeezed, and Loretta covered her chest and leaned against the fridge, speechless. Then she jumped onto his back.

"Hai-ya."

Dan's cigarettes were on the table and I slid one out of the package.

"I'll show you something," I said.

"What do you want to show me?"

"Something."

Dan tapped the corner of his cigarette pack against his cheek. I stood. I had nothing to show him. I would put my arms around him and lay my head against his chest. I would tell him I loved him. His hands would rest on the small of my back. He would love me, too.

He tapped his fingers against the table, reached for his fedora.

I led the way.

While I put my shoes on in the hallway, I heard Matthew say to Loretta, "Let go, lesbo."

"Lesbo?" Loretta's voice was high.

Dan said, "Everyone knows you're a lesbo."

Then, suddenly, Dan was in the hallway. He straightened a picture. "What are you going to show me?"

"Surprise," I said. I opened the front door.

Before I unlatched the gate to the backyard, I looked behind me to make sure Dan was following. He was, fingers slid into his front pants pocket. I realized in that instant that nothing I did or felt had anything to do with love. It was something else, deep down, that made me feel as if I had to do things, as if I had no choice.

I sat on the picnic table.

Dan stood in front of me, flicking his lighter repeatedly, and I smelled the clean smell of his jacket.

"It's a joke," I said. "I don't have a surprise."

"You have one."

"I don't."

"You dragged me out here for nothing?"

"I like your hands," I said. Then I felt dizzy; the alcohol was churning in my stomach.

"My hands?"

"They're nice."

"Anyone ever tell you, you're weird?" Dan said. He held his hands out before his eyes.

"I'm not weird," I said.

"Yeah," he said, "you are."

"I'm like everyone else."

"Trust me, you're not." He tapped a cigarette out of his shirt. His hands were less kind, more selfish.

"I'm older than I look."

"Stop making me laugh."

I told him I was not afraid to do anything, and as I said it, I felt it to be true.

"You mean you're not afraid to go scuba diving?"

"Other kinds of things."

"What do you want to do?" Dan said. His smoke rings shook.

"Things."

I lay on my back on the picnic table, which was cold and damp.

"I'm tired," I said. I closed my eyes.

"You're not weird," Dan said. I opened my eyes. Dan placed a hand on my forehead, then held it over my eyes. Then he slid it over my mouth.

"Your face is perfect," he said.

He drew his hand across my neck, down my chest, rested it on my left breast, then squeezed tightly, so that my skin burned.

Inside, I finished off the chocolate icing using a spoon so I could get a lot in my mouth. I found the whisky mug, empty.

I closed the bedroom door behind me and went down the hallway.

In the living room, Loretta had Matthew pinned, her legs holding down his arms. Every time he got a hand free, he gave Loretta a purple knurple, twisted her nipple.

Dan reclined in the easy chair, and all I could see was his shaking foot. I put on my mother's red coat, the one she always wanted me to wear whenever we went out to dinner, and I took my brother's package of cigarettes with me.

The air was cool, and I did not love it as much as I used to, the briskness, because a heaviness came with it, but I wanted to be alone, deeply alone. I tucked my hands inside the sleeves of my mother's coat. Where was she? On the end of a hotel bed, her hands gesturing, trying to reason with William? Or maybe she was saying, I give up. William would leave.

The song "Hot Knife Boogie," Dan's favourite, suddenly blared from inside the house, and this meant that everyone else was having fun, having fun without me.

The door opened.

"We're doing bottle tokes," Dan said, and he was smiling as if he were ashamed, hapless. He had touched me; he had shown that he wanted me.

"I don't do those."

"Suit yourself." He shut the screen door and the winter door behind him, so that the music was only a rumbling.

I zipped up my coat all the way to the neck to keep out the breeze, then brought my feet up on the chair. I had often seen my mother sit in this same chair when she said she felt down and needed to think, when things were not going how she wanted them to and she had to try to find a way to deal with it: she was an expert struggler. I straightened out my legs, gazed at them in their dark denim. In the next moment, I felt something happen in my body, something unusual that I had never felt before. I felt something slowly expand inside me, fill me from head to foot, making me taller, more solid, different, as if I were suddenly older, more capable. I wondered if this was how it felt to be a woman, if I had suddenly become one. I brought my legs up and hugged my knees tightly, watched the sky grow heavier.

WHITE CARPET

AFTER THE trip to Niagara Falls, Selena returned to my father and they lived together in his penthouse. Finally, she flew back to Montreal and my father never spoke of her leaving, never told why. I did know that, afterwards, my father wanted me to visit more. These visits grew sombre, strange, long. During car rides on unfamiliar roads, he would try to pass on what I detected was wisdom but could not decipher. He told me, for instance, never to punish myself, to leave that to God, never to make myself unhappy with guilt, to let go of the past. After paying for gas, he would slip money into my pockets, telling me never to refuse money. He touched me more, but without confidence; he would tap me gently on my forearm as I gazed out the car window, as if I were a gold statue in a museum and he did not have the right, only the need, to give me good wishes.

On the days I visited, he would pick me up and drive me to the apartment he had lived in since leaving our house when I was nine. Back then, I had adored the artificial bushel of roses, the framed photograph of a kitten—I had thought that he had chosen them for me. Now that I was fifteen, though, they struck me as funereal, too dusty, stiff.

At the apartment, if he did not snooze on the couch, he wore his thick glasses and sat at the kitchen table, where a college math book was open in the middle to long equations. He was trying to learn math so that he could become an engineer, and not what he was, a subway conductor, something I considered more glamorous, full of risk and death.

Sometimes, we would drive to downtown Toronto, park the car, then take the subway, and while we waited, my father would point out which trains were new, which ones he hated to conduct. I'd never seen him drive a train because he had never let me, though I'd begged; he said the conductor's booth was no place for a young girl. I couldn't imagine him at work. My father was different from the other drivers I had glimpsed through the glass, who all struck me as rotund, bleak, and somehow vicious. They were alien, belonging to the underground. My father's warm hand, his calm voice, made him too fine and gallant, too delicate to control a rumbling, thrusting, violent train. One time, as we were riding southbound to Queen Street station, he told me of the girl all in white whose arms and legs had been severed when she lay on the track. "I don't think she was expecting that," he said.

I liked to spend time with him because I was lonely too, trapped in delicate but indestructible netting. But I told no one, because it was worse than a private place, it was something I was doing wrong, something I couldn't seem to make right. As far as I let anyone know, I was an important girl in high school. He did not know that the girls who smelled of baby powder, the girls who plucked their eyebrows, ate toothpaste for fresh breath, were distant gods to me. That, instead, I was burdened with Loretta, her laugh that caused others to laugh at her, her brittle helmet of hair.

I believed final and secure acceptance would come to me through a white or black waist-length rabbit-fur jacket, through the use of hairspray, anything that could be purchased to improve my appearance. Without these aids, I felt constantly drizzled on, damp.

From my father's balcony, I had a view of a nearby high school, the large gravelled roof, the caged windows. I could imagine leading a perfect, simple, organized life inside those walls. And my father would never bother me. He wouldn't know me well enough to know how to get to me.

We were eating cereal and toast the day in January that I proposed to live with him. My father frowned tensely at his placemat, swallowed two bites of toast as I waited. Then he said it would be nice to have a girl around the apartment to keep him company. He said it would be nice to have someone to talk to at dinnertime. And then he said he would allow it if my mother did.

We set the date for moving in for the coming summer. My mother expressed shock and doubt at my father's sudden loyalty and devotion. "Lonely, is he?" She didn't forbid me because she said I would never go through with it, live with the man who had shown himself for what he was: selfish.

My father imported a bedroom suite from Germany, a red and white set that I could not believe would be mine. Not just a bed and a dresser, but a wall unit with a desk I could lock up. This was the room in which I would grow beautiful, as solid and gleaming as wood. He hung up white curtains, and he took the trouble to install a blind, one I loved to open and close on my visits. The room I deserved was waiting for me. So was the orange sherbet he had started buying for my visits after I had sampled it on a cone and decided impulsively, and without commitment, that it was my favourite.

My father once again took up smoking and he was determined to teach me chess, though I was too distractible a student. I made careless moves and didn't care when I lost; instead, I was relieved, I could stop pretending. After chess one day, he rooted through his closet to locate a book on airplane crashes. I read it intently, hunting for descriptions of death, hopelessness. I picked up knowledge haphazardly, when I wanted.

With me reading, and my father dusting or studying his math, the apartment took on a wholesome, irresistible silence—silence I thrived in. I could hear my thoughts clearly. Also, in the quiet and motionlessness, I was the only object to pay tribute to.

If he walked past me as I sat on his couch, he would pat my head, more confidently than before, as if he were now sure I would not bite.

"Hey, kiddo."

"Hi."

"How's my daughter?"

"Fine."

His apartment was the peaceful interior of a shell I entered; inside, nothing was wrong with me, nothing was abnormal or mournful. I stretched out my limbs with pride, with love for my body, with a thrill at how wonderful and flawless I was, strong.

One day, he drove me to his favourite road, the hilliest region in our town. From it, we could see cliffs and a creek far below, next to which my father had slept as a teenager when his mother had locked him out of the house for the night. She did this if he did not arrive home for his curfew, and he had kept a tent permanently hidden there. He had taken me to it before.

"That was where I slept," he said, rising in the car seat, trying to see.

"I know."

"Not in winter. Winter I made sure I was home for curfew. One time I saw a bear," he said. "I mean, I thought I saw a bear. The shadow of one. I could see its claws. Just a tree branch."

He patted my hand. "You're lucky you never have to sleep outside. I had a good time, though, sometimes. Out at night by myself. It wasn't always bad." And his description ended there, as if the experience had been pressed into a vague slate of pain.

A deep-down layer of me, one I often accessed in emergency, began to panic at the prospect of living with my father. Would I stand firmly in the new school, my back refusing to weaken with the always acute sensation that I had been sewn with inferior thread? I received terrifying flashes. My father would pull me down to the bottom of the ocean. He would make me become like him, someone unable to fight. Someone who struggled in the deeper, larger currents, who could not find a way up for essential air. He would clutch my hand. I would drown. This fate was not meant for me. Despite all my doubts, my intention was to be drenched in glory. I was to have my way.

"We could take a walk down there," he said. "I could show you the exact spot."

But my father's need of me was intoxicating. It blurred my vision, softened my thoughts. Peering into this face of need, I was reflected back immaculately, my holes filled in. The offer of someone's love is even more irresistible when you don't have to love back, when you can leave at a moment's notice, when you have not offered a shred of yourself in return.

I made the agonizing walk down with him.

Loretta and I, one lunch hour, decided we would defy fate, fight doom. We would attend a party before the end of the month, join the students who glided past our table to sit in a crowded area of the cafeteria, where the loud, confident kids were. We offered cigarettes to girls who we knew had talked about parties in French class, who told of people breaking windows, starting up lawn mowers in the middle of the night, stealing bras off girls by holding them down on the kitchen floor. Epileptic seizures. Girls convinced by boyfriends to eat dog bones, or their worst secret would be told.

I talked to one other girl besides Loretta. Her name was Ivonne, an unattrctive name that better suited an older woman, a woman with a car and a trench coat and a briefcase. I sat beside Ivonne in biology and she smelled faintly of urine, but strongly of new leather because she wore her black leather jacket to every class instead of leaving it in her locker. At lunchtime, Ivonne waited in the parking lot for her boyfriend, aged thirty-three, to pick her up in his truck. The boyfriend meant she did not have to put effort into forming alliances—she had been carried already into the other world.

I found out that Ivonne was the next-door neighbour to a girl, Marie, who worked in a clothing store and was having a party.

"Want to have lunch together?" I said to Ivonne, since biology was right before lunch.

"Jim might be coming."

"I'll wait with you, in case he doesn't come."

"Suit yourself."

"Loretta, too."

"Fine with me."

It was a day in January in which the breeze could actually be borne and the sun was out. Loretta ate a smelly peanut-butter sandwich, and I ate crackers and jam, the fastest thing I could make that morning.

"What are you doing on Friday?" I asked Ivonne.

"Marie's having a party. You guys coming?"

"Maybe," I said. "I'm not sure."

Ivonne squinted down the road; the lunch hour was almost over and there was no sign of Jim. "Stoned again," she said. She hadn't eaten anything.

I met Marie in the bathroom, where she was applying lipstick smoothly. Next, she drew a brown mole on her face, and that she knew exactly where to place it over-whelmed me.

"Ivonne invited me to your party," I said.

"Ivonne," she said. "Don't gross me out."

"Why'd you invite her?"

"Deborah is going to beat her head in." Then she looked at me, startled, and did something that amazed me. She took my two wrists into her hands. "Please, please, please don't say anything. I'll be your best bud for life."

"I wouldn't," I said, feeling my stomach twist and drop.

"God, your eyes are so blue," Marie said. "Oh my fucking God are they ever."

"Loretta's coming too."

"Beatty?"

I nodded.

"I mean it. You can't say anything to Ivonne."

"What did she do?"

"Had sex with Deb's boyfriend in Deb's car."

"Ivonne has a boyfriend."

"Ivonne is desperate. She'll fuck anything that walks."

Marie and I exited the bathroom and turned in

different directions down the hallway. As I shuffled as slowly as possible back to class, I wondered how badly Deborah would beat up Ivonne.

When my father called me to take me out for my Wednesday dinner, I told him I couldn't go because I had a toothache, which was partially true because I had one, or the inklings of one, the day before.

"Oh, that's all right," he said. "I've had a bit of an upset stomach today anyway."

"Sorry."

"Hey, what colour carpet do you want? The landlord's going to let me tear that stuff up. I was thinking a nice rose."

"I like white."

"White? It gets awful dirty."

"I've always wanted white."

"All right, then, I'll see what they have in white," he said, and I could tell he was writing it down. "Hey," he said, "how about lunch on Friday?"

"Can't."

"Monday?"

I couldn't say no again, so I said yes.

"I'll drop by and take you somewhere. What time do you get lunch?"

"Eleven-thirty."

When I hung up the phone, my mother asked me, White what?

"Carpet."

"He's putting down new carpet?"

My brother Matthew looked up from the newspaper, then down again. I had become the honoured child, wanted by both.

My mother wanted the name and address of the party. I gave her a false name, Lisa Terk, and the correct street, but the wrong street number. In addition, I gave her a made-up phone number.

Matthew, who looked more of age, had gone to the beer store for me the night before because he no longer cared what I did, and because I had promised to vacuum the basement for a month, his only chore. I had hidden the beer in my closet.

Loretta and I were not sophisticated enough to think of a cab, and we walked across the bridge in the cold, holding our scarves over our mouths, complaining about the snow that had got down our boots because we had taken the railroad tracks as a shortcut. With numb extremities, we got smart and called a taxi from the newly built gas station.

In the back of the cab, I said, "I don't think Deborah really likes Ivonne."

"Deborah's a slut."

"Do you think Marie is?"

"Undecided."

We paid the driver exact change, then stood outside the house, which was rumbling. I led the way.

Inside, everyone was on the main floor, which was furnished with only one black leather couch, a coffee table that had a puzzle encased in glass, a stereo system with five levels, and a fern in a basket in front of the window. The music made it instantly impossible for Loretta and I to hear each other. We found a spot beside the stereo where I opened the bag and gave us a beer each. Loretta slyly took an opener out of her sock, an arrangement we had considered carefully.

"I thought you were a loner," a tall boy with a long dog's face said. "I always see you alone."

"I have friends," I said, cheerfully.

"Yeah, me," Loretta said.

"One friend?"

I picked up our bag of beer and said, "Let's go find Marie."

"Bye, loner."

We had to push through people.

Marie and Deborah were drinking glasses of vodka on the couch. Deborah, who had blonde hair but severely arched black eyebrows, said, "Seen Ivonne?"

"No."

"I like your lipstick," I said to Marie.

"Fuchsia," she said. "My mother won't let me wear it out of the house."

Then Ivonne came. She stood beside us, her hair wet and ratty, but her heavy black eyeliner still intact.

"It's pissing freezing rain out there," she said. "I need a towel."

"Come," Marie said, taking her by the arm.

I studied Deborah for any sign of what she was about to do.

"Boring party or what. But then, what isn't boring," Deborah said.

"Seems all right to me," Loretta said. "If you don't mind a crowd."

A man with red hair and extremely pale skin sat down beside Deborah. The fact that he drank his beer from a glass mug and wore cowboy boots made me think he was older. Really looking at him, I realized I'd seen him before with Deborah and Deborah's boyfriend off school property.

"What are you looking at?" he said.

"Nothing." I smiled.

Then Ivonne came downstairs, her hair combed but still wet, and she plunked down on the couch between the man and Deborah. "How the hell are you?" Ivonne said to both of them.

Deborah and the man put their arms around Ivonne, who leaned back, smiling a masculine, good-natured smile.

Marie stood at the top of the stairs. "Deb? Can you come here? I need to talk to you."

As Deborah got up, the man with the red hair pinched her on the bum. She giggled, then went up the stairs. Marie closed the bathroom door on them.

I sat down and Loretta sat on my lap, a position that I had noticed was fashionable for girls.

"How come you don't have freckles?" Loretta said to the man.

"How come you have no eyebrows?"

Loretta laughed, looking at me.

Then Deborah came out of the bathroom and called him. Watching him climb the stairs, I saw a knife in his back pocket, and I developed goosebumps on my arms.

"So, how come you guys are dry?"

"Wasn't raining," Loretta said.

Having finished my beer, I looked over to the wall where I'd left the bag—gone. "I might go soon."

"Stay," Ivonne said.

They came out of the bathroom. Deborah hung her arm around the man with the red hair, her eyes red, her lids heavy.

"Ivonne," he said officially. "I'd like to talk to you."

"Sure," Ivonne said, shrugging.

"I wouldn't go," I said.

"I've known this guy for two years," she said. "He used to hang around Jim."

He held the door for her, and she went out on the back porch. Marie and Deborah followed and stood outside without coats, shivering.

The boy who had called me a loner sat down beside me.

"You would look better with blonde hair," he said. "Wouldn't she?"

"Beats me," Loretta said. "Blondes are all hookers, far as I'm concerned. Blondes have more fun? You're damn right they do."

I kept looking towards the back door, and I found it difficult to listen, concentrate.

"She's in space," I heard Loretta say.

Two boys on their way to the kitchen stopped at the open door and looked out.

"Holy shit," one said, leaning in closer.

Three boys coming up from downstairs and one girl with flat, long hair stopped to look. Then Marie came back in, her face desolate, stunned. She hugged a boy whose shirt was too big for him.

Loretta and I got up, squeezed in behind the others.

Ivonne was lying on the snowy ground on her stomach, and the man with red hair was kneeling over her, one knee on her back.

"Say you'll kiss her ass."

"Jim's going to kill you."

Deborah was crouched on the porch, her head down on her knees, rocking.

The tall boy who had called me a loner opened the door and crossed the porch. "What are you doing, pothead?"

Marie stepped outside again. "Let her up, before I call the cops."

But the man with red hair wasn't listening. He was rapt. He pushed his knee deeper into her back, then mushed her face in the snow.

She said something I could not quite make out. It might have been "Get off me."

He squished her face in the snow again.

"Stop it."

"Say it," he said.

Then he turned her over and threw snow in her face. He reached for his back pocket.

"Forget it," Deb said. "She was born a slut."

He threw snow in Ivonne's face one more time. Then he walked up the stairs into the back porch, through us, and out of the house. Ivonne lay in the snow, her arms at her sides. She did not turn her head to us; perhaps, out of some instinct, she was playing dead; the mortification would perhaps be less if she never saw our eyes and we did not see hers.

Marie was sitting on the couch staring blankly as the tall boy stroked her arm.

When Deborah came in, one of the boys said, "Mattress-back." Another said, "Slut." I'd seen these things written about her on the tampon machine in the girls' bathroom: she was said to have let three boys have sex with her on the pavement behind McDonald's when she was in grade nine. Although Deborah did not respond to what the boys said, she went out the front door without her coat, without her boots. No one went after her.

The house was clearing. Boys gathered beer, girls looked for purses. No one was looking outside at Ivonne, to see how she might be doing.

"We should help," Loretta said, doubtfully.

"Let's just go," I said.

We walked home on the icy streets.

I carried a black purse to school, one I had received from William for Christmas. It was alligator skin, and because of this I had never carried it before: there was something too confident about alligator skin, too foreign. Before this day, the purse had been too much the possession of a woman. As I went out the door, meeting the cold wind, my brother asked me if I was on my way to Yonge Street.

I didn't hide it in my locker. I was careful to carry the purse as if it were nothing but a hassle, definitely not a treasure, and it was not difficult for me to feign this attitude because I was a tremendous actress—I made myself up by the second. I appeared to take the purse for granted.

Marie stopped me in the front foyer to borrow a cigarette, and she offered me a piece of gum, told me to meet her for a break.

In the ten-minute break between the first two periods, Loretta and I stood with Marie in the smoking area. Ivonne had not come to school, and Deborah had shown up with what we concluded was a bruise drawn on with eyeliner to attract sympathy.

The fact that Marie wanted to meet me and Loretta at our lockers showed me that she had lost Deborah as a friend and needed new ones. I was being used, and I knew I could be thrown away. I knew that I would have to be on my best behaviour at all times, that I would have to lie and pretend and give.

It was agreed that we would spend lunch with Marie, but not in the cafeteria where you couldn't talk, Marie said, without being heard.

As it approached, I felt none of my usual gloom. I felt neutral.

The bell rang. I met Loretta and Marie in the smoking area. We walked slowly, as girls in groups always walked, to a convenience store. We stood outside the store in the wind and light snow the entire lunch hour, eating raisin cookies. We were talking about Ivonne. We were drunk on our analysis. How the situation had gotten out of hand. He was only supposed to threaten her, Marie assured us. But he had liked Deborah, and

Deborah had used him to get back at Ivonne. And Deborah knew, she *knew*, that he had been known to act crazy. He had once challenged Jim to a race to see who could get a pint of blood out of their arm first by using a knife. She should have known, Marie admitted, but he had promised that he would only threaten. And the bottom line, she said—and we listened carefully for the bottom line—the bottom line was that Deborah's boyfriend had fooled around on *her*. Deborah should have been mad at *him*. But Deborah would do anything for her boyfriend. And Marie swore us to secrecy about what she was going to reveal. She even let him—and Deborah had told Marie this herself, acting as if she had enjoyed it—she even let him shove a beer bottle up her. Of course, Loretta and I would never tell anyone. And I wouldn't have. I could not have said those words aloud, though I relished them, turned them over in my head. We had to go back for lunch.

We were walking towards the front doors when I saw something that made my skin cold with shame: my father was standing across the road, his hand cupped over his eyes, shielding the sun, looking for me. He spotted me, waved, then simply stood there smiling.

"I have to go," I told Loretta. "My father."

"What's he doing here?"

"Never mind."

I had to let several cars go by before I was able to cross; as I approached him, I tried to conceal my humiliation. I could see his car, and on top of it was a long roll of carpet, tied and wrapped in plastic.

"What are you doing here?"

"We had a lunch date," he said.

I looked at my small watch on its black leather strap. "The bell's going to go."

He lifted the folds of his collar so that they protected his neck from the steel wind. He pulled back the sleeve of his ski jacket and gazed at his large, digital watch, his mouth shrinking as he appeared to calculate. He tapped the face of it.

"What time do you finish?"

"Three-thirty."

"I'll be back. You must be hungry when you finish."

The bell rang.

"I'll wait. I'll meet you right here," my father said.

"Bye." As I was about to cross the street, my father grasped my hand. "Maybe we'll have some dessert, too."

"Maybe."

I crossed the street and joined the colourful swarm of ski jackets.

I was anxious sitting in class, could not concentrate, and I eyed the clock or looked out on the schoolyard. Loretta and I met up again in geography, and as she was complaining about the sickly-sweet smell of someone's deodorant, I saw my father walking around the track, his head down, sipping a coffee. He was putting off his hunger for me.

I knew this was something that was supposed to endear him to me, but, watching him, I felt only that he wanted too much from me, that he would not leave me alone. I could never live with him.

When I was eleven, he had believed I would become a fashion model, and had taken me to a fashion show in the Eaton Centre. When the fashion show was over, my father had become possessed with the idea of buying me a dress. We took the escalator up to the girls' department in Eaton's, and he picked out a sailor's dress that had a navy, pleated skirt and short sleeves. He told me I would look tremendous in it, a real young woman. I tried it on in the change room and my legs resembled sticks; the shoulders of the dress were tight and uncomfortable.

He opened the change room door.

"We're buying it. You're a knockout."

"I don't like it."

"Beautiful," he had said, shaking his head. "Why doesn't your mother dress you in clothes like this?" He shut the door on my protest and I changed into my own clothes, clothes my body relaxed in, could breathe in. When I brought the dress out on the hanger, my father was talking to a salesgirl. "She doesn't want to be pretty."

After he had bought it, we went to a food court. "Go try it on," my father had said, indicating the bathroom.

"I'm not wearing it."

"You want a spanking?"

I had consented, to avoid disgrace—I knew he would try to do it.

He waited at the table while I went into the bathroom, which contained only one other person. She was drying her hands under the dryer, and I envied her for doing whatever she wanted, when and how she wanted. I pulled the dress on in a cubicle, then sat on the toilet. I couldn't be seen, and at that moment, I became the girl

I truly was. I stood, pulled the dress off my head, and balled it into my hands. I would not wear the dress, I would not wear it for anything. I pushed it down the toilet with my hands, then my foot, to make sure it was soaked. I flushed the toilet, but it only gurgled, and the bowl overflowed, began to flood. I passed one woman and a baby on the way out.

I then rejoined my father. I told him the dress had fallen in. He said I would get a spanking, but drove me straight home, instead, not talking to me. Before I got out of the car, he said if I wanted to look scraggly, that was my choice. "Not everyone can be a model."

At three-thirty, I walked stiffly from the school to his car, which was idling in the cold. The wind had picked up, and I felt somewhat relieved to be inside; but there was the fact that I did not want to move in with him, the idea of it gave me no pleasure. In fact, I would be missing out on things, on goodbyes, invitations, revelations about other girls, borrowed brushes, warnings, compliments. All the elements of the kind of friendships I wanted. All the elements along the road to becoming essential. I panicked slightly as we drove by a crowd of students and I saw the back of Marie's jacket.

"I thought I'd make a nice winter stew," he said.

"A winter stew?"

He slapped his hand down on his knee. "Jeez," he said. "Did I tell you? I failed that damn course. The woman beside me hardly ever came to class, and she passed."

"You failed?"

"Thinking a little too highly of myself, I guess." He turned up the heat. "I don't know if we'll put that carpet down tonight," he said. "I can't believe you made me buy white. I said to the guy, 'This is for my daughter. She has to have white.'" He laughed. "He says his daughter has to have a ruffle around her bed. Daughters." He smiled, brushed my cheek with his finger.

"It didn't have to be white," I said. And then I couldn't hold it in, I had to chop everything down all at once, so it would be done. "I'm not going to live with you." I hadn't even meant to say that. I had meant to say "can't," and then follow it with an excuse.

"What?"

"I'm not," I said.

"What? Of course you are."

"I'm not."

He tapped my knee. "Come on, what's this about?"

"I have friends," I said. "I can't leave them."

"Friends?"

At that moment, I knew it wasn't true, that they were not friends, that I had tricked myself into another kind of loneliness. But I was too far in to get out.

"Jeez," he said. "The room's all fixed up. There's curtains. Blinds. That's all for you. Waiting for you."

"I'm not," I said.

"Boy," my father said, "you really pulled the wool over my eyes."

"I didn't mean to," I said, tightly.

"You sure did a good job of that. Boy oh boy."

We were almost to my house. The windows were dark; no one was home. But I still wanted to get inside.

I still didn't want to live with my father. He needed me too much.

"I guess I'll take the carpet back," he said, and I could tell he was trying to threaten, trying to show me that my decision was final.

"I guess you'll have to."

"I was all set to put it down tomorrow."

"You'll have to take it back."

"Tomorrow morning. First thing. The salesman will think I'm a nut."

We were parked in my driveway. I opened the car door.

"I guess I can't believe what you say anymore," he said.

I looked at him, into his angry, wrung-out face. Into the face of the man who was supposed to be my father, and who I tried to believe was. Perhaps it was the time of day, the sky growing dark grey, but all at once I saw everything in a way I had never before. He was a stranger who struggled to know me. I felt a collapse of something, an anxious stem of caring, an anxious stem of caring that had grown up some time before, during my sleep. It collapsed, and I was left with a feeling of independence, a necessary separation. It satisfied me to be cut off, to cut others off. It satisified me to be hard.

"I never wanted to," I said.

"That's too bad," he said.

"Goodbye."

"Well, goodbye."

As always, he waited until I was inside before he left. I went to the window to watch the small car go, followed it up the street with my eyes.

BLIZZARD

I LEANED below the graduate portraits and waited for Loretta to be dropped off by her mother, who worked at ABC Donuts. I also watched out for Tuk, who was in my math and history classes and had missed four days of school in a row. Since September, I had phoned him at home.

Loretta, wearing high-heeled black boots, floated through the front doors carrying a bag of sugar donuts.

"Study?" she said, her nose red from the cold.

"I might go home," I said.

"We have an exam."

"I'm failing anyway."

"You have to pull up your mark."

We bobbed through the crowd towards the smoking area.

I stopped outside my locker, and my hands were tingling and numb.

"I'm going."

Loretta produced a white sugar donut out of her bag. "Did you eat your breakfast?"

I zipped my coat and retied my scarf, too thin for the cold. "Yes," I said.

"You're going to miss so much that you're going to fail everything."

I thought of the geography exam, for which I'd studied only two hours and knew everything we'd learned. There would be rows of students beneath strips of fluorescent lights.

"I'll phone you later," I said.

"You just want to go home and talk to him because you know he'll be home."

"No."

Loretta told me that I was pathetic, that I acted like a little puppy, always calling him, that he didn't even like me enough to call me for a change.

I did the thing we had promised never to do: I walked away from her, leaving her alone and helpless and therefore a spectacle in the middle of the hallway. She would have to fend for herself.

William had taken time off his job as a sprinkler salesman to start his own sprinkler business. My mother had told me that he was the best sprinkler man in the country and might even become a millionaire.

I opened the front door with my key. The house was quiet except for the sound of hot air blowing through the vents. I had to sit down on the landing that had just recently been carpeted to pull off my boots. The slush from the roads had leaked through two identical cracks in the heels. But the boots were grey suede, moon boots, rising just three inches above my ankle, and I had to wear them; they were the one pair of boots I had ever been proud of.

I was pulling off a wet sock when I heard papers rustle, the click of a pen. William cleared his throat: his throat was chronically phlegmy, and I had noticed, since his return two years before, that he cleared his throat once a minute, sometimes twice a minute.

I had barely spoken to William in two years because, by the time he had decided to return to my mother, I had a different opinion of him. Not speaking to him was a way of hurting him for ever leaving her at all. I was wiser than I had been before he left. I had, though, spoken to him once. I had asked him to drive me to the mall because my mother was at euchre, and I was meeting Loretta outside of Grenada, a restaurant, so we could pretend to be nineteen and order Bloody Marys. He had agreed to drive me and we had said nothing to each other in the car except goodbye.

Once my socks were off, I stepped into the kitchen to get something to eat. Since William had returned, the fridge had been fuller. We had even started a food cupboard in the hallway.

He sat at the dining room table, writing something in pencil. The table, bought by William, was covered with loose pieces of paper; a typewriter stood at the end for my mother's use in the evenings. She typed what he had written.

I took out two pieces of bread from the bag, buttered

them with margarine that was already on the counter. The side of my body that faced William was tense.

He cleared his throat. I looked at him, but his head was down and he bit his lips. My mother had told me that William wanted to talk to me, but I wouldn't let him because of the grudge I was holding.

"I'm not feeling well," I said. "That's why I'm home."

"Did you say something?"

"I'm home because I'm not feeling well."

"Tell your mother," William said, writing again. I could tell he was pressing hard.

Instead of taking an orange and a glass of milk from the fridge, which I wanted to do because I was hungry, I took only the buttered bread into my room so that I would not have to spend more time near William. My room was chilly. I sat on my bed and pulled the satin quilt over my legs. It was still early in the morning and the sun reflected like a metal plate. The most interaction I would risk was going downstairs to watch television later.

On my dresser sat a red phone that William had bought me for Christmas. Christmas was another time we spoke, to say thank you.

I phoned Tuk and he answered on the fourth ring.

"Hi," I said.

"Who is this?"

"Leah."

"What do you want?"

"To say hi."

"Hi."

I asked Tuk what he was doing, and he said he was practising his guitar; he practised four hours a day. The amp had put his mother three thousand dollars in debt.

"You haven't been in school," I said.

"I'm finished," he said. "You know what?"

"What?"

"I got to practise. I'll phone you later."

"Okay."

I said goodbye, hung up. I believed he would call me because, the week before, he had glanced at me as we stood for the national anthem, glanced and smiled, as if he wanted to know me. He would call me and my life would take shape. I would be cared for; he would tell me I was important, love me.

I got up and stood at my window. Everything was lit up, and I wished I was outside.

"I think I'm hemorrhaging," my mother said, feeling between her legs. "It's that time of the month." She added, "Janet from euchre hemorrhaged, you know."

We were driving home from the mall at the centre of town. My mother had just bought me a winter jacket, one that cost over a hundred dollars, filled with down. She had bought a pair of heeled cream boots for herself, just under a hundred dollars. Our prizes were in the back seat.

"Are you going to die?" I said, letting out a breath.

"People have," my mother said. "But you don't want to hear about it."

"I don't."

My mother positioned the car in a long line of cars waiting to exit the mall parking lot.

"Other daughters act a little more grateful. I heard a girl in there tonight say, 'Thanks, Mom.'"

"Thank you," I said.

"Say it like you mean it."

"Thank you, Mom."

"You're not happy," my mother said. She said she remembered what it was like to be my age, but that I had to get through it. She slammed on the brakes suddenly, smacked the steering wheel with the side of her fist. "Christ," she said. My mother, breathing more urgently, her hands tense around the wheel, did not continue the conversation.

"Someone might call me tonight," I said.

"Oh," my mother said. "Who?"

"Someone," I said.

"Who?"

It was finally our turn to exit the parking lot.

"This person."

"A boy?" my mother said.

I nodded.

"Who?"

"Just this boy."

"Do you like him?" she said.

I told my mother no, I didn't, but that he liked me.

She asked me his name, and when I told her, she tasted it, then said, "Funny." She told me I could tell him I got a new coat.

"While we're on the subject," she said, "how about saying something to William? Do you know what it feels like to have my daughter walk out of the room every time the man I love enters it?"

"I have nothing to say."

"Say, 'Hi, William, how was your day?'" She imitated a cheerful voice. "I mean," she said, "what did William ever do to you?"

We were driving across the bridge, and I glanced down at the traffic below, rushing.

As we pulled into the driveway, my mother said, "All right, here's your chance. What are you going to say?"

"I'll ask him how he is."

"That'll open it up." She told me she always knew I had it in me. She smiled triumphantly.

My mother opened the door and we were suddenly surrounded by heat. William came immediately from the bedroom into the hallway.

"What did my lady buy?" he said.

"Some boots," my mother said.

I took my boots off slowly.

"Will you have some cashews?" William said to my mother, offering his palm.

"Cashews," my mother said. "I love cashews." She licked her lips theatrically. "Cashew, my sweet?" She offered me her palm, but the nuts struck me as deathly, items dug up.

I did not look at William's face; I couldn't remember the last time I had actually seen his eyes. They were bright blue, pained. They startled me when I met them, and I suddenly felt there was too much light in the room, too much feeling. Nothing would ever be said.

I brushed past my mother, brushed past William, and went into my own room, shut the door. I put the coat on, lay on my side on the bed, but I was still cold. I heard them go into the kitchen, the clatter of plates, utensils.

In the seat beside me, Loretta wrote every math equation from the board into her notebook. I stared out the window, which was level with the ground covered in hard snow. Tuk would just be getting up out of bed, a waterbed he had told me about the first time I had phoned him. The night before, I had fallen asleep with my clothes on, waiting for the phone to ring.

I wrote Loretta a note to say that I was going to do better in school so that I could go to university, because I wanted to be rich.

She wrote back that it was too little too late and she'd heard it all before. At lunch, we stood in the smoking area, just the two of us, shivering among larger groups of leather.

"You're spaced out," Loretta said.

"I have things to think about."

"Like having sex."

Loretta and I had started a race to see who could have sex first, and I had not yet won.

"No."

"He's what you live for."

"No, he isn't."

"You dream about him twenty-four hours a day."

"No, I don't."

"I'm getting sick of you," Loretta said. "You're not even a friend."

"I'm a friend."

"When's the last time you called me?" She blew smoke in my face. "You just use me so you'll have someone to hang out with."

Loretta dropped her cigarette on the pavement, stepped on it. Professional, she withdrew another.

"See you," she said. In her heels, she stepped towards a group of girls whose hair was stiff with hairspray. A girl with red hair even said hello to her.

It was a cold, bright day. Without getting my books from my locker, I left the school through the front doors, confidently and firmly, so that I would not be questioned. I kept my shoulders back until I reached the intersection that marked the end of school property.

I passed a group of students who seemed eager to get back, to end their break.

When I got to the next intersection, I was out of the wind. I was on the very highway that Tuk lived on, and I tried to calculate how long it would take me to get to his house, tried to imagine the distance. Without making a decision, I started walking in that direction. I had never been there, but I knew he lived across from Knob Hill Farms, and I had seen his house when my mother and I went shopping.

The walk was longer than I thought, and I could no longer feel my toes. To keep calm, I breathed deeply through my nose, thought of my body below my skin, the warm blood, organs. When I got to his place, there were two German shepherds running around a blue car that was in the snow-covered driveway. I stood at the end of it. When the dogs ran around to the back of the house, I went up to the front door. I could see into the living room, but it was empty, just two couches facing each other.

I knocked. Just as I thought no one was home, Tuk answered in his jeans. He had a white shirt on, the sleeves rolled to his elbows, something I would never have imagined.

He frowned when he saw me, licked his lips slowly, thoughtfully.

"Hey," he said. "You look cold."

"I came to say hi," I said.

"Hi."

"Can I come in?" I said.

"You'd be bored," he said. "We're jamming."

A sudden wind came up, making the windows clatter, and I put my mittened hand over my mouth.

"I wouldn't be," I said. "I like jamming."

Tuk kept his hand on the heavy door. I smelled chicken cooking.

"Downstairs," he said, and I stepped in, feeling more frozen than I had been before he opened the door.

On the way downstairs, he let the dogs in the back door and they knocked me into the wall as they passed me. Tuk walked ahead of me, his shoulders slightly hunched, like an ape's. Downstairs, a tall blond man gazed at me with curious disdain, rapidly hitting his drums.

I kneeled on the floor. They were playing heavy metal. Before he had left school, Tuk had made me a tape and I played it as I fell asleep. It was an hour before they stopped completely. The blond man, who squinted at me, said, "I never knew a chick who liked to watch

jamming." He put on a ski jacket, said he would see Tuk
on Sunday. He went upstairs and dog claws skittered on
the floor above me.

"That was good," I said.

"I was a bit slow," Tuk said.

He sat on the couch beside me. He told me that while
he'd been playing, he'd come up with an idea for a
rocket that was powered by water.

"Yeah," I said, wanting to get on to the true subject:
whether or not we would be together and whether or
not we always would be.

He set the drumsticks beside him on the couch. He
narrowed his eyes at me, frowned, concerned.

"I'll tell you," he said. "I don't want to hurt you."

"You're not going to."

"I might," he said.

"You won't."

He closed his full lips thoughtfully. "You're a very
open girl," he said.

"I am?"

"You call me almost every day."

"Because I like talking to you."

He paused, took a cigarette from behind his ear,
looked at it, then replaced it.

"You don't have to be afraid of me," he said.

"I'm not."

Tuk leaned into me, but I automatically turned my
head away towards the wall panel. When I looked at
him, he glanced at my top.

"Pink," he said. "You look good in pink." He rubbed
my arm with two fingers.

Though I no longer wanted to kiss Tuk, I leaned into him. His mouth was slimy, sour, and I tasted smoke.

Afterwards, he sighed, sat back on the leather couch, and closed his eyes, rested his hands on his stomach.

"Leah," he said, and that was my name.

Before anyone else was awake, I smoked one of my mother's cigarettes, a Vantage, at the living room window. Snow blew and piled.

The school had called my mother, and she was driving me there to make sure I went.

"I want to know who this boy is you call," my mother said. "Is he telling you not to go?"

"No," I said.

"Sometimes boys think of themselves first, Leah. Their sexual urges. They can't help it."

"He doesn't tell me not to go."

"He might influence you without your knowing it."

The car trembled because of the wind. We were approaching the school, and I felt my breakfast rise up in my throat, but I swallowed it down.

"You can't miss any more school," my mother said. "You need this year, Leah. I'm not kidding. I wish I was."

She idled outside the building. Her hair was freshly curled and she smelled of perfume, for work.

She clasped my wrist. "You look pretty today," she said. "Your eyebrows are nice."

"Thank you." When I got out of the car, I wished that I was the girl who had coughed all through grade nine and had eventually died.

Inside, the halls were empty and I found my locker, scanned my schedule, retrieved my math and geography books. Something was different. I could not see the end of the day.

I climbed the stairs to geography and stood outside the classroom. The teacher said something about the layers of the earth, but I didn't care, what he said was distant.

I descended the stairs, which smelled of floor cleaner and damp, and peered through the rectangular window on the door. I saw the track almost covered in snow. Trees bent in the wind. I had a choice. I could stay at school and wait for the bus and get home safely, or I could walk home through the snow and wind, experience the assault of the elements. Loretta had learned to live without me; there was no obligation to stay by her side at lunch. I hoped she would be sorry she had scolded me, but I knew I was guilty, that I thought of Tuk more than her, more than school.

After dumping my books in my locker, I put on my coat and left through the front door. I had left my mittens at home and kept my hands in my pockets.

On the bridge, I was almost blown over. The wind blew my hair to one side, completely off my face, and wet snow blew into my eyes. At the intersection, I held on to a pole to keep from being knocked down. My hair was wet, knotted. A car pulled up beside me and a teenaged girl looked into my face with concern. I stood straight to look strong, unbothered, but my eyes were watering from the cold.

Off the bridge, I walked in the direction of the lake, and the wind pushed me every few steps.

Though William was inside, the door was locked and I had left my key in my other jeans, so I had to climb through the front window, scrape my stomach on the sill. William found me when I was still on my knees, knocking over a plant. He pointed a sword brought from his travels.

"What in hell?"

"I'm sick."

Without speaking, I stepped to my room. William wouldn't dare enter my room. I heard him yank the vacuum from the hall closet, lug it into the living room.

I lay on my bed and my skin grew warm. Beneath my eyelids were flashes of the highway below the bridge.

I called using the red phone in my room, and Tuk answered on the second ring.

"What?"

"I thought you might want to come over."

"It's snowing."

"I'll make it worth your while."

"I don't got a way over there."

"Cab."

Tuk sighed. I remembered ten dollars in my long coat, change I owed my mother.

"I'll pay."

He told me to give him an hour.

I showered, put on my pink robe and stayed in it. I blow-dried my hair, then I went out and made a peanut-butter and lettuce sandwich, ate it in large bites in my room, then lay on my side and gazed at my digital clock radio. In a matter of minutes, my life would be different—simple and proper. I would be a girl who had

been wanted, a girl whom a boy had wanted to be
with—and this meant that anyone who believed I was
not special would be wrong. I would look down on the
other girls, and whatever I wished to receive would be
given because I had been selected and pursued. It was the
most crucial moment of my life.

The vacuum cleaner died, the cord was wrapped up,
and the house was quiet.

Soon, the doorbell buzzed, and I stepped carefully to
the door, as if trying not to break something.

I gave Tuk the ten-dollar bill, and as he turned to pay
the cab driver, the smell of his shampoo mingled with
the cold.

William worked at the dining room table. I hoped he
would hear. He would see that someone cared for me,
that I was a chosen girl, one that someone had to have,
couldn't live without. I led Tuk into my bedroom and
closed the door. We sat on the floor beside my bed.

"You smell like soap," he said.

I bent my knees and one poked through my robe.

"I like robes," Tuk said.

He rubbed my bare foot. "Small feet."

I kissed his whiskers, then his neck. Soon we were on
the bed and beneath my brown bedspread.

"I'm starting to like you," Tuk said.

I opened my robe. Tuk pulled down his jeans. His face
was in the pillow when I felt the first shove, and the pain
was a razor, and another razor, another, and then it was
good and I knew I was bigger than he was, and stronger,
and that he could never hurt me.

★

When my mother came home, she told me that the school had called. I had been asked not to finish my year because I was failing every subject and had been absent as much as I had been present. The principal wanted to see me the next day to sign papers.

"This means you're looking for a job first thing tomorrow," my mother said.

I told my mother I was glad, closed the door of my room. As soon as I did, my ears grew hot, my head pounded.

Outside my room, my mother and William talked in the hallway. I heard my mother say that I would have to talk to someone, a professional, because I was confused. William murmured, "Yes."

I had no one to call. The only person I thought of was my father, but I did not know his number off by heart, and I would not know what to say.

My mother knocked on my door, opened it hesitantly. "Leah, I think it's time you got straightened out. Talked to someone."

"I'm fine."

"You feel sad."

"I'm happy."

"I don't believe that."

I smiled for my mother, told her that, really, I had never been happier, that I was happy school was over.

She squinted at me. "You are?"

"I am."

"Where are you going to look for work?"

"The bowling alley," I said.

My mother told me that was a good idea, there were other kids that worked there too.

"You'll go back," she said. "I know my daughter. You've got something special."

At that moment, I felt I would not move backwards or forwards; I was gripped by something inside me, urges, impulses, wishes, portents of disaster. But I nodded.

She came to my bed, put her hand on my hair.

"You're certainly not dumb," she said. Then, standing, she said, "Shame. Maybe you can start over at the school with the nuns. Come out if you feel like talking." She closed the door. There was despair in her voice, her posture. She must have known there was nothing she could do now, only watch.

My mother had to go into work early, so it was arranged that William would drive me to school. I showered and William bathed. When he finished his cereal, he asked me if I was ready and I said yes.

We had to warm up the car before we could pull out, and as we waited, I tried to harden myself, to stop from shivering. I had never failed so awfully in my life, never done something that could not be fixed. I felt as if something that had been surrounding and protecting me had been lifted away, and I was exposed. I had become someone entirely new, someone who could not get away with things, someone who had to work harder for everything. Nothing would be given.

We pulled out, and everything I had been feeling made me want to talk to William because I wanted what was between us to be over. If I had nothing else, I could at least have a stepfather who spoke to me, whom I spoke to. Eventually, he would buy me a blue dress, something I would look beautiful in, and he would show me his country, England, that he had left long ago. I would no longer want to shut him out.

He switched on the radio and that was the only sound. Yesterday's snow had packed tight and the air was thinner. On the highway, William drove slowly, both hands on the wheel.

"I guess my life is over," I said.

"Not necessarily," William said. "People can make extraordinary turnarounds."

That was it and I believed him. William had been to university, a distant one, and he knew things, and now he cared. It was not over; there was hope.

He could have driven the car faster, more dangerously. I was cared about. I wanted to go to another school and I wanted to do well and I wanted to bring home A's. I would become something respectable—a noble scientist.

Sooner than I expected, we were in the parking lot of the school.

I could make everyone happy, and I could make things right.

I said something I didn't mean. "I love you."

William's face appeared to have been struck—his eyes widened and he looked at me as if he had never seen me before.

"I'll be waiting out here," he said.

I opened the door, my muscles braced automatically in the cold, and I made my way.

SURVIVORS

ALEC MOVED in with us when his mother could no longer handle him, when he was out of control. He was in the grade I would have been in, and nobody would say what he had done. I imagined him trying to strangle Sharon, his mother. Getting out of the car, he was tall and wore a bewildered expression that I found disturbing.

My mother forced my brother Matthew to help with the boxes, though there were only two. I helped carry in clothes, still on hangers. My mother supervised with a cigarette held between two fingers.

"Don't look so gloomy, Alec," she said, rubbing his back.

Alec stepped away from her hand.

William rubbed his red palms together whenever he passed Alec. "You excited, my boy?"

When the boxes were in, William sawed and nailed wood in the basement because we were turning the back half of the laundry room into a bedroom.

Late at night, as I lay on my bedroom floor, I heard William say that he was going to buy Alec a waterbed and install a mirror closet.

I went downstairs, feeling oddly excited. I wanted to talk to Matthew, not about anything in particular, but because we never talked anymore. On the way to his room, I accidentally caught Alec standing in the rec room in just a white shirt, pale thighs like stems. He was getting ready to go to bed on the couch.

"Oops."

"Doesn't matter."

I stepped down the hall, dark because the light had burnt out and knocked on Matthew's door, which was heavier than any other door in the house. He opened it wearing the expensive blue terry-cloth robe I had made my mother buy for him.

"Can I come in?"

"Why?"

"To talk."

"About what?"

"Something."

"What?"

There was so much to talk about, I couldn't choose.

"I don't feel like it," he said.

"Fine."

He closed his door, and I felt a keen loss of hope. But there was Alec, and it was like remembering a new coat, the one that would change everything that needed to be changed. I would talk to him and he would listen, thinking of nothing else.

In the rec room, he lay on his back on the couch with

his feet up, wrapped up to the neck in a blue comforter that my father had bought for my bed, one that seemed better than other blankets, as if it possessed special knowledge and abilities.

"Do you want the light out?"

"No."

"I can show you around."

"I used to live here."

"I'll walk you to the bus."

"No, thanks."

"Night."

Alec did not say good night, only smiled. I flicked out the light anyway and climbed the stairs, full of energy.

On a Saturday night, when only Alec and I were home, our parents took us out for Chinese food. I hoped someone would see me in the car with Alec beside me because then others would know that I had access to a brother who thought highly of me without my having to work at it. Throughout the drive, my mother caressed the nape of William's neck.

"Do you have your homework done, my boy?"

"No."

"You'll end up crying on Sunday night."

Alec pressed the side of his face against the window, and I wondered if William hated Alec, if he wished he hadn't been born. He'd been excited when Alec had first come, but since then, he'd been trying to make Alec into someone like him: someone who could be the owner of a business.

When we parked at the Silver Dragon, Alec kept his seat belt on and his eyes closed. "I'm tired," he said.

William opened the back door. "Up you get, Alec. Don't be a baby now."

Alec rested his head against the back seat, his mouth hanging open, and William pulled his ear until he was sitting up straight.

"You'll eat your dinner, my boy."

After undoing his seat belt, sighing, Alec shuffled to the door of the Silver Dragon, ten feet behind us. It was quiet inside. A waitress came out from behind a door and smiled, revealing brown teeth. The empty tables, covered in pink tablecloths as thin as icing, made me sit down very delicately, to fit into the mood, not disrupt it. Alec sat down, leaned back in the chair, crossed his slender arms, and closed his eyes.

"Alec," William said. "Alec."

"He's fine," my mother said.

Alec rose and entered the men's bathroom. The waitress with brown teeth and a full smile came and we ordered soup for all of us, including Alec. He was still in the bathroom when our jiggling bowls of soup arrived. When William stood, my mother held his right shirt cuff.

"Leave him," she said.

While he ate, William stared into his soup. "He'll get hungry."

We were waiting for the waitress when Alec emerged from the bathroom, looking refreshed, as if nothing were wrong.

"Let me order something for you," my mother said, stretching her neck to try to spot the waitress.

"I just want soup," Alec said. He slurped a spoonful, causing my mother to flinch.

"Leah has a famous appetite," William said.

Though I rarely ate with them, I liked the idea that something was known about me.

"I'm having everything," I said.

My mother frowned at me, detached, as if she were the judge and I were the criminal.

"Leah's a sport," William said.

"Just hungry. Can we drink?"

"No," my mother said, blowing out a match. She loved laws.

"I think Leah can handle a glass of wine," William said.

"Can I have some?" Alec said.

"But Alec," William said, politely, "wine is for men. You've done nothing but demonstrate that you are a baby."

My mother rubbed Alec's back. "I'll pour you some of mine."

William snapped his fingers for the waitress, who put down a cloth on the counter where she was standing. He ordered me a glass of wine while my mother stared critically at the tablecloth, arranging her chopsticks. I tried not to look at Alec. My mother ordered the food and the waitress left with our menus.

Alec zipped his jacket and headed for the entrance.

A waiter tried to show him where the bathroom was, but Alec opened the door and floated through. I stood up to follow. I would soothe him. "Finish your soup," my mother said.

Then she and William turned to the window, which was draped in pink curtains. Alec was walking with his hands in his pockets towards the intersection, his dark head a stain.

"It's a nice night." She sighed. "Looks like he's going home, anyway."

"It is a nice night," William said.

We all looked out the window. Finally, the waitress came with our wine. William poured my glass. I drank several sips at once, but the taste was disappointing, bitter. When the waitress brought the food, William and my mother picked at it. I finished mine first.

At last, they laid their chopsticks to rest.

On the way home, my mother kept her window down to smoke and I sat on William's side to avoid the breeze. I rested my hands on my stomach, which had expanded, making my jeans tight, and I kept my eyes open for Alec.

"Maybe he'll decide he wants to go back to Sharon," William said.

"Well, Sharon won't be too pleased."

"Sharon's never pleased," William said. "Maybe she'll take him back. Alec has to do what Alec has to do." He drove with two hands on the wheel, energized. "He's a survivor, eh?"

My mother exhaled out the window. We passed a lone person on the sidewalk, carrying a coat, and William slowed the car, then sped up. It was a girl.

The rest of the way, I felt the narrowness of the streets, how they hugged the traffic. There was still an expectant tension in the air, something that was being thought but not said.

When we pulled up the driveway, rattling the sewers, Alec was just getting out of a cab.

On Monday mornings, I worked in a bowling alley minding the children of women who bowled. I organized games and snacks for nineteen children under the age of five, one only two months old. Every time I left, I hoped something would happen so that I would never have to go back.

This Monday, I was home by twelve and the house smelled of Alec's body odour. For the few weeks that he had been here, he had recoiled from fresh water and soap, but embraced tea, fruit, and Player's Lights. In the evenings, when William tried to help him with his math homework, Alec would whine and resist so loudly I could hear him in my bedroom. "You'll never become anyone if you do not pay attention, my boy," William would say. Then Alec would quiet down, and if I went out to the kitchen and caught a look at him, his face would wear a determined, violent sulk. When William discovered that Alec was not attending school regularly, he told him he was securing his destiny as a failure.

In the living room, he was lying back in William's easy chair, a banana peel on the arm. After the dinner at the Chinese restaurant, my mother had told me that Alec was not right upstairs, but I thought he acted strangely because his mother had kicked him out and we did not yet love him. I thought he did not go to school because, when you did not feel at home, everywhere else was the landscape of a nightmare, empty, labyrinthine, full of unexpected, bloody battles.

"Why are you home?" I said.

"Missed the bus."

"Want to go for a drive?"

"Huh?"

"Do you want to go for a drive?"

"Why?"

"To see things."

"All right," he said, his voice higher.

I decided to explore the outer edge of town, which I barely knew myself. The Malibu was William's car, and my mother had told me that he had decided to give it to me. I wore her black leather gloves, which she had forgotten that morning. Wearing them, I became some-one who did what she wanted.

I warmed up the car and Alec sat beside me. When I glanced at him, he smiled at me in a way that was too grateful, lit up. A small wave of warning began to form and grow in the back of my mind, a wave of uneasiness. But I smiled cheerfully, generously.

I backed out, then drove, holding the wheel lightly.

"Do you like it here?" I said.

"I might hitchhike up to Barrie."

"I would never move."

Because there was no traffic, we glided through the town, beyond it. On a long road where a different kind of people lived, the people who owned Ski-Doos and

motorbikes, we drove past the stable where my mother
had once forced me to ride a horse because the neighbour's daughter rode.

"Want to drive?"

"No licence."

"No one will see."

The car felt like a boat on water as I carefully pulled
over to the shoulder of the road. As Alec and I switched
sides, his hand pressed down on my thigh. In the passen-
ger seat, I immediately felt off balance. He drove with
one limp hand on the wheel.

"Holy," he said, accelerating.

"Be careful," I said. "Someone died up here." In a
motorcycle crash, her face had been scraped off.

"Relax," Alec said, speeding up, and even the engine
sounded terrified for itself, humming at its limit. Alec
swerved towards a woman with a rolled-up red umbrella
and swerved away just in time, laughing. "I could have
got her."

"Pull over."

"Afraid?" He smiled at me with unbrushed teeth.
Then he caressed the side of my head, kept his hand
there, and I knew what he thought: that, out of some
mutual desperation, we would provide for each other,
that he liked me and I liked him. The wave in the back
of my brain expanded and I saw what he was—someone
who sucked blood. Someone who sucked blood so
eagerly, it was repulsive.

I yanked his hair and the car shook, and I yanked it
again and in one second we were nose down in the

ditch, the car still running. Alec, whose eyebrow was bleeding, looked at me as if it were my fault. I had been wearing a seat belt.

I took the gloves off because I was suddenly hot. I used both feet to shove open the door. Outside, I pushed on the front fender, trying to move the car, and my back and legs began to ache. I could see Alec through the front windshield and he was simply sitting behind the wheel.

"Get out here," I said.

Though there was a glare on the windshield, I could see his face, hollow, long, how a face looked when it was absorbing horrible facts.

I started to walk down the long road, the shoulders covered with leaves. I searched my pockets for change, found a skimpy palmful.

Before I turned a corner, I looked back and Alec was still sitting in the Malibu. I wanted to go back to save the car because I knew it would be difficult to explain to my mother how I had allowed the accident to happen, and what I had been doing in a car with Alec. Doubt would be cast on me; I would not be trusted. But I did not want to give him the satisfaction of going back to him. I despised Alec now. I wanted to punish him, and I wanted him to be sorry he had ever known me.

When mother and William arrived home from work, Alec had still not returned. I had to tell them about the car; I had to tell them that Alec was not back.

"What do you mean, he's not back?" William said.

"I don't know where he is."

"Don't know where he is?" my mother said.

"I left him because he wouldn't help."

"Is he all right?" William said.

My mother cut in. "Was there any blood?"

"Only on his forehead."

William phoned the police. We would meet them where I said the car had gone into the ditch, report the accident, then report Alec as missing.

On the drive to pick up the car, my mother asked me one question: "Were you going fast?"

"He was."

The police arrived before we did, a man and a blonde woman with a ponytail. First, I told them how it had happened, and they wrote it down, the woman looking up to check my face. "Did you get into a fight?"

"No."

All of us searched the area to make sure that Alec, possibly hurt and disoriented, had not stumbled off, fallen. Later, William and I gave a description of him. William gave the officers a small picture that he had in his wallet.

When William asked what could be done, the policeman said they would file a report and assign a detective, but unless Alec was a risk to himself or others, they could only list him as a missing person. They would not search. He said to phone everyone Alec might know.

The car was towed. The police left.

On the way home, William said, "If it were their child, they would have the whole force on it. They're useless, I tell you. They're a waste of money. They're a bunch of useless apes parading around, wielding power over everyone. Useless."

"Yes," my mother said.

Later, William went out to look. My mother suggested I accompany him because I had better eyes. We took the Grand Prix, and he wouldn't start the engine until my seat belt was on.

We drove so slowly through the streets, people must have thought we were criminals. Then we drove to the high school, and William got out and circled it on foot while I sat in the car slowly zipping and unzipping one of my new leather boots. Anything new was a direct product of William's hard work, but I never thanked him. These boots were part of the person I was turning myself into, a person who walked without doubt, slept without doubt; but I had not yet achieved this. Uncertainty was a flat, vexing taste in my mouth. By the time he returned, the wind had reddened his cheeks and his face was tight with cold. We drove along the road where Alec had driven the car into the ditch, the empty road where trees hid everything.

"Nowhere," I said, and suddenly shivered. "It was just an accident."

We went farther out of town, and I entertained the idea that William had lost his way and we would have to drive all night, searching. But soon the Silver Dragon came into view, the lumber store.

William rubbed his eyes. "He'll be home," he said. "I'll bet you anything that he'll be home right now."

At that moment, we saw a boy on the shoulder of the

road. He wore a red and black lumber jacket like Alec's.
William hastily pulled over. Cars honked, cars that may
have been filled with people who knew me, kids I had
known at school whom I could not, without warning
and preparation, face.

William got out, his mouth set like a satisfied hunter's,
and jogged towards this boy. As they talked, their white
breath escaped. After a moment, the boy slung a knapsack
over his shoulder, and William put his hands in his pockets and came back to the car. I felt sucked into the outside
world when he opened the door, then sealed in again.

"Not him?"

William cleared his throat. My mother had told me
that men cried, but I had only seen boys. I studied him
with quick looks, his thin face, vulnerable as cotton.

Before bed each night, I drank hot milk to subdue my
brain, which produced wires of thought. Alec had been
gone for a week, and William and Sharon, who called
nightly, had contacted everyone Alec knew and found
nothing. William made it a habit to go out and look. My
mother told him Alec would come home when he
wanted to, but William said Alec could get into some
kind of trouble.

"He's probably in someone's house. Hiding. Not on
the streets."

"I'll find my son," he said. "You leave that to me."

She did.

One night, I sipped my milk as Matthew and my
mother spoke in the living room. Late-night whispered

conversations were a constant between them, and it was the closest I saw my mother to being in love.

I leaned against the living room wall.

"I'll kill him," Matthew said.

"Who?"

"Are you a part of this conversation?"

"Leah," my mother whispered. "Not everything concerns you."

Matthew butted out his cigarette, kissed my mother good night, and passed me without a word. Since he had grown muscular, his walk had changed, as if he were perpetually defending himself. Lately, the sight of me triggered a disgusted expression on his face and a stomp out of the room.

On her lap, my mother had a loosely knit red and black blanket, stolen from a family reunion, and a pillow to support her neck, taken from her bedroom.

"Why are you sleeping out here?"

"Who says I am?"

"You look like you are."

"I may fall asleep." She held a flame to her cigarette. "Is it so hard to sit with your mother in the dark?"

I nodded.

"One day you'll realize I'm the truest friend you have."

And this was unthinkable, that I would rely on her, want to hear what she said. A friend was someone you thought better than yourself. Leaving her, I felt what I always felt, that there were hooks in my shoulders, pulling me back to her.

★

The next Monday, when I was finished at the bowling alley, I rode the Dial-a-Bus home. Alec was already there, eating a pepperoni sandwich—pepperoni was something my mother bought strictly for herself. She sliced it on crackers with cheese, and I could anticipate her disappointment. Someone had once again undermined one of her few pleasures. The kitchen smelled of body odour, and a cold wind was blowing through the living room window, which Alec must have opened. The sheers filled and the drapes escaped their ties, and I felt unsettled, imagining the grimness of my mother's face if she were to enter the chaos.

"Did you go to Toronto?"

"No."

"Barrie?"

"I'm staying in my friend's basement."

He had left the last inch of pepperoni unwrapped on the counter.

I poured myself a glass of orange juice that was slightly sour. Alec wiped his mouth with a serviette—the British upbringing.

"You took all the pepperoni," I said. "That's my mother's special food."

"She can get more."

"But it's just for her."

"She can get more," he said. "My dad pays."

"No, he doesn't."

He stopped chewing and gazed at me sympathetically, as if I were sad, naive, the last to know. As if I were pathetic, and as if he were older, knowing more.

"You can't stay here."

"It's my dad's house."

"He doesn't want you here."

"I'm going to pay for the damage."

"It was too much." Then I paused for a moment. "He said it was just like you to do this. He said there was no hope for you."

Now his long, pale face was sorrowful, and I imagined what it must feel like to be him. It made me want to be meaner.

Alec set down the complete half of his sandwich.

I stood on the landing while he put on his shoes, tied his runners that would let in the slush. Would there ever come a time when I would lose control? When I wouldn't be able to save myself?

"I like you," Alec said.

I waved, though he was standing right there.

WAITRESS

THE SUBWAY car was empty, except for one man with shaggy hair and a gym bag between his legs. I was on my way to work downtown, though I was only seventeen. I wanted to sing professionally. I wanted to do something that no one expected of me, something that would show who I truly was.

I brought exquisite dishes to a group of men with trim haircuts, shaved faces, plush briefcases. A thin man with black hair, a flat cap of curls, rested his hand on my back as he ordered smoked cod.

When only the man with black hair was left at the table, I hovered around the flower arrangement like a fly. I was yanking a rotted freesia bloom from its stem when a flash went off. The man who had put his hand on my back held a camera. He stood close enough for me to smell his breath.

"Using up the last of my film," he said. His hair looked soaked. He took my hand and pressed the picture, not yet developed, into my palm.

"Thank you," I said.

"You don't live in Toronto," he said.

"No," I said.

He smiled, pulled on his earlobe.

"You're from the outskirts, I bet."

"West Hill," I said.

"I'm not from around here, either," he said. "Louisiana native."

He picked a flower bloom, an alstroemeria.

"You like waitressing?" he said.

"No," I said. "Not really."

"How old are you? Sixteen? Seventeen?"

"Almost eighteen," I said.

He smiled at me without speaking.

"I want to be a singer," I said.

"Astonishing," he said.

He picked another bloom, a freesia, and brought it to his lips.

"Eat much?" he said, glancing at my waist. "You have the body of a twelve-year-old."

"Yeah," I said, which was the truth. I moved around the table, hoping he would leave.

"That was rude of me," he said.

"I have to work," I said. "Bye."

"Bye?"

"Have to work."

"You're an interesting young lady," he said. "You want to be a singer. Have you ever been to the opera?"

"No."

"I could get tickets."

"No, thanks," I said. This time I stepped towards the kitchen. "Bye." I waved, strolled through the door with the freesia petals disintegrating in the heat of my hand.

I gave my mother a portion of my paycheque for rent, but I was saving money for a piano so that I could learn how to play, then sing songs, become known. And this is how I'd been imagining the path of my life since it had occurred to me, in my days out of school, that I did not want to be ordinary.

My mother encouraged me to consider my options. I should scout around for a manager's position, something to suit my brain. I didn't want to be taking orders all my life.

But the future was a pleasant, fragile blur. I would entertain in a lounge, my voice curling up the walls.

Because it was a warm day, the kind that came suddenly at the end of winter, then disappeared, my mother carried her coffee onto the patio where I was already reading *The Wandering Jew*, a book I had found in the basement. My mother snuggled in a blue velour house-coat, a gift from a euchre friend, which made her skin look younger, her eyes swollen instead of dry, shrinking.

"How was work?" my mother said. "Any interesting episodes?"

"Slaving," I said. "The usual."

"Slaving," my mother said, turning the page of the newspaper. "I don't know if I'd call it that."

"Serving other people is slaving."

"Fine," she said. "Slave all you like. But a situation is what you make it." She met my eyes.

"Some man asked me out," I said.

"Some man?"

"Some guy," I said. "This guy I served."

"Well," my mother said. "And what did you say?"

"No."

"No?"

"No."

"How old?"

"Forty," I said. "Or so."

My mother thought about this for a second. "That doesn't sound right. A forty-year-old wants a date with you?"

"I said no."

William, his hair wet from bathing, opened the screen door and informed her that the bathroom was free.

"Thank you," she said, without looking at him. They had hardly ever looked at each other since Alec had left, because, according to my mother, William had closed himself off and made the search for Alec his full-time job.

By the time I got to the restaurant, my stomach was empty. I rinsed dishes in a large white laundry tub under water that burned my fingers. When I was through, I went to check on the flowers in the dining room.

The man I had seen the day before sat at a table with a cup and saucer and a newspaper not yet opened.

I collected empty coffee cups from the patio. I was

crumpling a napkin in my hand when he was suddenly behind me, a black blazer over his white silk shirt, unbuttoned. His skin was tanned, gave off a smell of garlic, and isolated black hairs crept around his collarbone.

"I bet your name is Cynthia," he said. "You look like a Cynthia."

"Leah," I said.

He told me his name was Roy. "Worst name in the family."

"Yeah."

"Do you get lunch?"

"No," I said, lying, "I only get a fifteen-minute break."

"For all day?"

I nodded. He asked me when I got off.

"Late."

"Late," he said. "You must be hungry when you get off."

"Usually," I said. "I eat when I get home."

"That's a long way home."

"I read."

He asked me what I was reading. When I told him, he said he had never heard of it.

"You probably go home to your boyfriend," he said.

I said nothing, so that he wouldn't know.

"How about dinner with me," he said. "When you get off work. Like seafood?"

Though I did not want to be with him, the thought of spending part of the evening in Toronto, with its lights and cars, people that pushed, appealed to me. At home, I would be missed.

"I don't eat seafood," I said.

"Italian?"

"I eat that," I said. "Most of the time."

He asked me what time I got off and I told him. I waved goodbye with a cloth in my hand; he laughed.

I waited outside against the brick wall, which was draped with dead ivy. The restaurant was busier than it had been earlier. It was colder, and to pass the time, I counted sidewalk stones that I could see near the road from where I stood.

Women with large heads and stiff hair hung on to the arms of men. I deeply breathed in the smell of perfume as they walked by me, opened the heavy wooden door to go inside. The smell made me want to close my eyes and allow the world to pass without a contribution from me, without a whisper.

He rounded the corner, carrying his black dress jacket over one arm. His lips, precise and red, were barely visible beneath his black moustache.

"They wore you out," he said.

"Yeah."

"You like saying that."

"What?"

"'Yeah.'"

Resting his hand on the small of my back, he told me that when he had heard me say it in the restaurant, he had found it endearing. The hand was heavy iron, weighing on me.

"We'll have to see where we can squeeze you in."

"Squeeze me in?"

"Dress code."

My breath became shallow. I was wearing good jeans, a leather coat I had received for Christmas on a promise to go back to school.

"I'll eat anything," I said, pulling away from his arm. "I don't care."

He slipped both of his hands into his pants pockets.

"You'll eat anything," he said, tasting the words, resigned.

The wind blew my hair out of my face on the way to the small Italian restaurant, which had dark windows, dried pots of flowers on the outside. Inside, the carpet was the colour of squished roses, and the room was quiet.

The waitress led us to a table in the centre of the room. When we were seated, she smiled at me briskly, carefully, as if trying not to see me.

"It's quiet," I said.

Roy asked me if I wanted to go.

"No."

He opened his menu with long, hairy fingers. I suddenly imagined those fingers against the skin of my stomach and could feel myself gag. I opened my menu and noticed my own fingers with unfiled nails, unpolished, the skin dry.

"You don't like this place," he said.

"It's okay," I said.

"You're beautiful when you smile."

The waitress poured us water.

"Sing for me," he said, choosing a bread stick.

I told him I was not ready.

"Not ready?" he said. "You either can or you can't."

"I will when I'm ready."

He gazed at me, chewing the bread. "You're very stubborn," he said. "That's very appealing."

Then he told me he was a contractor, and when I asked him what that was, he told me he was in charge of buildings, seeing them built.

"Do you live in a shoebox?" he said. "You don't know what a contractor is?"

"No, I don't live in a shoebox."

When the waitress came, I ordered spaghetti because I did not want a surprise. I wondered what would happen if I missed the last train out, whether Roy would drive me home.

He ordered clams in sauce.

"You like seafood," I said.

"Yes," he said, "I do." He folded his hands together and peered straight into my eyes. "Can't get enough of it."

His eyes fell briefly to my chest, then rose to my head.

"I like the way you do your hair," he said.

"Thank you."

He laid a napkin across his lap and I did the same.

The waitress brought a carafe of red wine. I thought she must have known I wasn't old enough, but maybe in Toronto, when you were with a man, there were special rules.

"It's nice to be drinking wine with a beautiful girl," he said.

Though I knew he was referring to me, I thought he must have been seeing someone else in his mind.

After dinner, he drove me to Union Station. My legs slipped against the black leather interior of his car.

"You don't say much," he said, switching on the heat. "That's not good."

"What do you want me to say?"

"I had a lovely time." He picked up my fingers.

"Dinner was good."

"Dinner was good," he said. Then he dropped my fingers, leaned his head on the headrest, and laughed. His neck was long and blemished, and I decided that no woman had ever desired him.

"Bye," I said, opening the car door. Union Station glowed.

"See you in two weeks," he said. "I'm away on business."

"Bye," I said, slamming the door. As I descended the steps, his car idled behind me.

When I got home, the front door was open and my mother was waiting for me in the dark living room.

"They kept you late?" she said. The cinder of her cigarette lowered to the ashtray.

"I had a date," I said, removing my leather shoes.

"A date with the older man?"

"Yes," I said.

"Is he nice?"

"He's nice."

"From Toronto?"

"Louisiana."

"Did he drive you home?"

"To the train station."

"Is he with someone?" my mother said, rolling the ash off the end of her cigarette.

"Why would he be with someone?"

"Some men like to have a side dish with their main meal."

I told my mother I was going to bed. I had to rise at six, to go in for a morning shift, late night or not.

I left my coat on the couch, threw my shoes down onto the landing, entered the bathroom to wash my face. I ran cold water because I remembered that my hairdresser had told me that cold water closed the pores.

My mother lightly knocked. Then, without waiting for a reply, she opened the door.

"I would hate to see anyone take advantage, that's all I'm saying, Leah." She glanced at her own reflection in the clean mirror, assessing.

"I haven't told you about Norma," my mother said.

According to my mother, Norma, whom I had spent every day with in grades five and six, had recently spent two weeks on the psych ward because of a man's deceitfulness: he had fooled around. She had swallowed a bottle of aspirins.

"I'm not Norma."

She lifted my hair, pulled it into a loose ponytail, held it with her hands. The touch of my mother's fingers provided temporary sanctuary: nothing mattered for those seconds.

"I'm just telling you what I know from experience," she said. She dropped my hair and we were separate again.

"I'll decide."

"Do you feel lonely? Is that why you want to date him?"

"I'm not lonely."

"Everyone gets lonely. Even I do."

Instead of replying, I lathered my face. I stared into my own eyes until I felt my mother look away, resigned. When she went into her room, she left the door open a crack, a narrow hand. She did this when William was away for the night.

When William came back from his business trip, my mother wanted him to throw away the bell-bottoms and shirts he had had before his first marriage. I heard my mother slide open his mirror closet, the rustle of a garbage bag.

I looked through the living room window and snow was melting.

I wanted to move to Toronto, to have my own apartment, where I would come home from singing in a lounge, my body relaxed. Someone would have to hear me sing.

I found my mother in her room and asked her to come into mine, and I shut the door behind us. Her face was suspicious, ready for bad news, something ludicrous and horrible.

"I want you to listen," I said.

"Listen to what?"

"Me, sing."

"Are you sure?"

"Yes."

"Let's hear it." She stood holding her two hands together, as if posing for a picture.

I took a breath because I had been told that this was crucial. But my throat stubbornly produced no sound.

I took another breath, this time deeper. I exhaled a note, somewhere around A, and my voice barely hit the wall or left my body. I took another breath because I wanted to get it out.

This time, I tried a song; I had the ugliest determination. I sang the first one that came into my head, "Blowin' In The Wind." I stared at the wall above her head, and my face grew hotter and hotter. Singing, I sounded only slightly different from when I spoke, just gentler.

When I was finished, she said, "Keep practising."

She closed the door behind her.

I shut my eyes, let my head rock against the subway window. Roy's skin lost its red blotches, his arms were less hairy, and his mouth and chin adopted a firmness.

On the way to work, my boots became soaked with slush.

At work, I watched out for him. When the restaurant was empty, I pruned the flower arrangement, searching far into the stalks for sickly leaves.

His stubble had thickened, giving strength to his jaw. He sat at a table near the door with a woman wearing a knee-length striped skirt. When he smiled at me, his lips were a chewed red. He ordered coffee for both of them, and the woman smiled at me with a long, dark mouth. When I brought their cups, I said, "Do you want anything else?"

"No, thank you," he said. To the woman, he introduced me as his friend, Leah.

I went back to the flower arrangement, from where I could see the side of his face, large arc of nose. I stared until he stared. Roy gazed out the window and then he turned his gaze to me, where it stayed, curious, puzzled. I stared back, my spine elongating.

Before they left, Roy put his hands between my shoulder blades as I wiped a table. Because he had startled me, he seemed suddenly taller.

"Would you like to go for a walk later?" he said. "When do you get off?"

"A walk?" I said. "Okay, I think."

"You think?"

"I mean, okay."

Behind him, the blonde woman was standing at the door, tracing the toe of her long boot along the pattern in the carpet.

He gripped my fingers. "See you," he said. The skin around his mouth wrinkled. I allowed him to hold my hand.

He leaned against the brick wall.

"How's the waitress?" he said.

"Fine," I said.

"Just fine?"

"Where are we walking?"

"I thought we'd drive." His black car sat like a beetle around the corner.

The interior was clean, empty of debris. The black leather paled Roy. "I prefer heat to cold. What about you?"

"Heat, I guess."

I was immediately lost in Toronto. People, arrogant and enclosed, with mouths hidden in scarves, pushed along sidewalks, risked traffic. I could see myself living among them, slipping in, seen only when I chose, living invisibly.

Roy took tight corners.

He rested his hand on my leg. "Did you really want to go for a walk?"

I let out a deep breath. "No."

He asked me if I had ever seen the quieter parts of Toronto. His apartment was in a quiet area, and he could see Lake Ontario from his kitchen window. The thought of his kitchen made it safe: I saw us eating strawberries, then me getting up to go.

We drove in silence, and I stared at pedestrians.

His apartment building glimmered like a gold earring. After sliding through the gate, Roy parked us underground. Though we had not spoken, I sensed a conversation.

"The last time I saw you, your bangs were puffier," he said.

"So?"

"That seems to be how the girls wear it."

"So?"

Roy said that he had not meant to rile me. Strolling

through the parking lot to the elevator, neither of us spoke, but Roy touched the small of my back. At that moment, he seemed to be the only person who knew me, my only link.

The mirrors in the elevator were dim, absorbing blemishes, lines of anxiety.

"You look worried," Roy said. "Am I worrying you?"

"No."

Hand on my back, he directed me out of the elevator. The hallway had a pinched smell of vegetables, deodorized carpet.

"You're not talking," he said.

"You're not talking either."

He laughed, squeezing my nose. I pushed his hand away from my face and he quickly said, "I'm out of touch."

Inside the apartment, I kept my boots on, though he took his off. He turned on the kitchen light. The room was clean, except for one bowl and one glass in the sink, a loaf of brown bread on the counter.

"Hungry?" he said. "I've got fruit."

"No," I said, though I had eaten only a muffin in two hours.

He bit into a green apple. Then he found a bottle of wine in the cupboard above the sink. He poured two glasses.

In the living room, his couch was patterned with large red roses. The only other place to sit was a wooden rocking chair, so I chose the couch. Roy sat beside me.

"You like wearing skirts?" he said.

"Sometimes."

"I used to have a girlfriend who never wore jeans. It was against her religion. She wore skirts."

He rested his hand on my leg.

"The wine's good," I said.

"You're not old enough to drink." Roy gulped, let a breath out of his nose. "What do you like about an old man?"

"You're not old."

"I'm old."

From beneath his stereo, he took out a photo album. He held it on our laps and flipped the pages. In one picture, he played the keyboard with a sulky expression, family members around him. In another, he was bearded, his cheeks red with acne. He told me that the picture had been taken just after he had been released from jail for possession of pot.

"Jail?" I said.

"Eighteen months." He looked into his wine. Then he smiled at me. "Ever thought you'd go out with a jail-bird?" He finished the wine.

"No."

He leaned into me, his hand lying low across my stomach.

"Can I see the rest of your apartment?"

The bathroom was small, with a white mat and shower curtain. He had a spare room, holding an exercise bike with a towel draped across it. He turned the lights on in his bedroom. Instead of a blanket or bedspread, only sheets covered his bed. He switched out the light. In the dark, his eyes were fierce, wrinkled, animal.

He peered at me, puzzled. Then he gripped my shoulders roughly.

"You need to relax," he said.

It occurred to me that I was not doing what I was supposed to be doing. Something was wrong with me.

I touched a button on his shirt. "Plaid," I said. "Plaid is nice."

Roy gazed at me as though from a dangerous height.

"I'm not a good man," he said, taking a deep breath.

"Yes, you are."

He picked up my hand and rubbed it between his own until my hand was hot and numb.

We stared at each other.

Roy bent to kiss me, his moustache scratching, and I knew I did not want him near me. His long arms squeezed me as though I were a pillow, something it had been his luck to find. He lifted me over to the bed, lay on top of me. His face, eyes closed, reminded me of an infant's, contentedly drinking.

I only kissed him, and didn't touch. His tongue was scratchy, cold, and I realized he was a stranger, complete and total. Then he untucked my top, felt underneath it, and something else took over, and I forgot who he was.

Instead of dropping me at the train station, Roy drove me along the 401 home. The 401 was almost empty; cars sped past us, each one containing a peculiar life that would never be known, just as mine might never be known.

The moonlight caught the hair on Roy's knuckles.

He would not remember me forever, and I wanted to pretend that I had done nothing.

"You're quite a woman," he said.

"Girl."

"Woman." His face hung bleak, as if something were dying before his eyes.

"You can drop me off at the top of the street."

"Right."

I considered work the next day. Would he come in to see me?

"Will I see you tomorrow?"

Roy sighed. "Maybe. I'm feeling pretty weird."

"Then I won't."

We drove off the highway, and Roy needed directions to my house. My town became a miniature town, the houses like shoulders.

He stopped at the top of my street. "Thank you," he said.

I experienced an urge to hug him tightly, close my eyes and have him become what I wanted. Instead, I smiled right into his face. "You're welcome," I said. His face was old. Getting out of the car, I began to feel different. After slamming the door, I was different. My boots crunched on the grass of familiar lawns and I knew that I could do whatever I wanted for as long as I lived and I would never be hurt. I would plough over people and never look back. The cold air melted on my face, and I strode briskly towards my home, my breath visible.

BAHAMAS

My mother hugged the duffle bag on her lap, her mouth grim as she eyed the bus driver. When she turned to me, she smiled, her lips dry.

"It's nice, just the two of us."

Tree branches clattered against the window. I chipped off old nail polish.

"Don't," my mother said, stilling my hand. "It's unattractive."

I tucked my nails into my palm.

In the hotel room, we shared a double bed.

Settling in, my mother hung up a single dress, red and black, an item she carried on overnight business trips with William. Red buoyed her up.

"Aren't you excited?" my mother said, running water in the bathroom.

She trailed out, wearing her summer robe, brown silk, bought in a boutique in Italy with William. Lying on her side, she lit up a cigarette.

"Here we are in Bahamas," she said, exhaling. "Come sit on the bed, hon."

I kneeled behind her and we watched it get darker. "In Toronto, it's cold right now." She wrapped her arms around herself. "We'll have some adventures tomorrow."

Then she pulled back the thin blanket, slid under the covers, removed her glasses. Without them, her eyes were large and imploring.

I changed, washed my face and brushed my teeth, then slid beneath the covers.

She sighed, clicked out the lamp reluctantly; I couldn't tell if she wanted to go out instead.

I opened my eyes and watched my mother's back rise and fall as she breathed.

After a few minutes, she rose without speaking, sat in the chair with her legs crossed, lit up a cigarette, blew smoke gently towards the window, her ankle turning.

She suggested a drink in the morning, since we were on holiday and time was different. "Not everything has to be how it is at home." She was wearing a hot pink strapless lounge piece. She adjusted her wide straw hat.

We stood in line at a bar and behind us were five young obese women speaking with New Jersey accents.

"I'm going to have the Bahama Mama," my mother said. "Bahama Mama," she sang, nudging me.

We carried our pink, foamy drinks out onto the beach. White lounge chairs lined the sand and we found two empty in the middle. Beside us lay a man with thinning blond hair.

"Drink up." She sipped, then licked her lips, as if she had come a barren distance. After pouring sunscreen on her arms and legs, she passed me the bottle.

I smoothed sunscreen onto my legs, feet, toes. Then I did my arms, the back of my neck.

Just as outdoor bingo began, the man with blond hair woke up and peered around him, dazed. He unbuttoned his orange shirt, revealing a narrow chest.

"Have you tested the water?" my mother said.

"Sure." He smacked his lips, which were full and hid an overbite. "You must hail from the north."

"T.O.," my mother said, which was her usual lie when no one would know the difference. Her only experience of Toronto had been when she attended secretarial school for one year. "What do you do?"

"Maple Leaf Gardens," he said. "Maintenance."

"Leah has been to concerts there," she said.

He nodded, squinting at me.

"A long time ago," I said.

He squirted baby oil onto his legs, then his arms, rubbed it onto his shoulders, luxuriously.

"Have you been there?" he said, oiling his chest.

"Me?" my mother said. "Not recently."

He offered her his baby oil, and my mother said she was already greased up, indicating her legs.

"So you are. You girls look thirsty," he said, standing in jean shorts. He shook sand from his white feet before he shoved them into sandals.

"We haven't finished these," she said, sipping.

"Guzzle."

When he was out of earshot, my mother said, "Don't you like him?"

"He does maintenance."

"What do you do?"

She assessed his belongings, picked up an orange shirt, smelled it, investigating.

When he came back, he passed over the drinks with long, trembling fingers. Then he sat down, grunted in relief, smiled with large yellow teeth, a tireless host.

"You're going to the club later?" he asked, but in an assuming tone.

"The club?" my mother said.

"You have to go to the club," he said, shooting out his hand to both of us. "Jerry."

We shook his hand.

"Dinner," he said. "Dancing."

"The club," my mother said.

"You two ladies have to have some fun while you're here." He grasped my mother's shoulder. "Live it up."

"I've done my share of that," she said.

"I bet you have."

"I'm going for a swim," I said.

"Don't drown."

Jerry told me not to swallow any of the water, because it was salt. I swam past a girl my age who was stomach down on a surfboard. I wished that I had brought a bikini, that I had thick hair and lips that someone could not resist. On shore, my mother peeled off her sun hat.

★

It was still light outside when we lined up for dinner at
the club. My mother, wearing her red dress with sandals
she had bought from the gift shop, flicked her ashes into
a fern. She strained her neck. "He said eight o'clock."

When it was our turn to be seated, the club was almost
full. I spotted him at a table in the corner of the room,
surrounded by occupied tables. A short waiter ushered us
outside, where the air was cool. He brought us water
and my mother sipped thirstily. "Keep your eyes on the
salad bar."

She drummed her fingers on the table, spotted with
someone else's crumbs. She inhaled deeply, exhaled in
agitation.

"Lovely," she said, pressing the glass into a napkin.
The wine reddened her lips, and this made me think of
William. One day when they were at work he had given
her a card and had written in it that he loved her.

"Why didn't William come?"

"Next time, if there is a next time, you ask him to
come."

The man rose and lined up at the salad bar with a
small, empty bowl. He shuffled into place with a slight
slouch.

"He's there."

"Where?"

"Salad bar."

She zipped her black purse, tucked the strap over her
arm. "I feel like a salad."

I followed her to the salad bar. A child, a boy in an
oversized top and oversized shorts, stood between us and
Jerry.

"The pickings," my mother said, her voice carrying to others in the lineup.

She reached across the boy and tugged Jerry's black leather vest.

"You've got some sun," my mother said to him, as if catching a ball at the last second.

"I do?"

"On the cheeks," she said, touching her own.

He felt his cheeks. "Burnt," he said. It was his turn to select food, and he stabbed the tossed salad with tongs, his hand sprinkled with blond hair.

As we waited for our bowls, my mother's eyes darted over the different foods.

After dinner, the small round tables were cleared away, moved aside to allow dancing. The music was rapid beats delivered like punches in the ear. A man in white pants spun records in the corner. On stage, a limbo contest played out.

"I pity the sole traveller," my mother said. "All the way from home and no one to talk to. He's about your age, too. Jerry."

"I might talk to him."

She waved to someone behind me.

Jerry brought strawberry daiquiris for my mother and me. His overbite must have made it difficult for him to close his mouth all the way, but in the dark, he took on a sexual strength, a decency—he would know what to do. He sat backwards on a chair.

"What do you have there?" my mother said.

"Tequila."

"Rough business," she said. "Tequila makes me tired."

"Not you."

"In my old age."

"What old age?" He reached across the table and picked up my mother's hand, smiled, resembling a dog. "These aren't the hands of an old woman."

"Jerry," my mother said, "how many of those have you had?"

He scratched his stomach, reached for his cigarettes out of his leather vest pocket, offered my mother one.

"You're thirty-nine at the most," he said. "I mean, tops."

"Ha."

"You're still a girl, for crying out loud." Then he told her that he had thought she was from Europe, that she looked European.

"No more tequila for you," my mother said, smiling brightly, tensely at me, as if we were on camera, under glaring lights.

"Do you have to wear a uniform?" I said.

"What?"

"Do you have to wear a uniform. At work."

"Yeah," he said, raising his voice over the music, so it sounded high, whiny. "I'm trying to get into college. For sound engineering."

I had heard of this program, and it gave him new nobility. He could focus, solve minute discrepancies. He possessed a complicated intelligence that would ensure his success. He would not crave my support and I could keep to myself.

A slow, frail song came through the amplifiers. Jerry pushed back his chair and stood behind my mother, picked up both her arms from behind. "Would you like to dance with me?"

"No, thanks, Jerry."

"Come on."

"No, thank you."

"Please."

"I'm digesting."

He pressed his chin on her shoulder. "Pretty please."

"To get rid of you."

There was no one else dancing and the floor was dark. She danced with an arm around his shoulder; he kept his arm around her waist. They held hands. Then Jerry put both his arms around her waist and she put both her arms around his neck.

At the end of the night, when my mother's legs were wobbly and her lipstick had melted off her lips, Jerry held on to her hand. She had to pull her hand out of his and she managed to do it, still smiling.

Later, we lay in bed, the lights out. Beside me, her breathing was short, jagged, the breathing of an older woman. At home, she rose in the middle of the night to have a cigarette, sometimes a swallow of vodka, which she sipped slowly, making it last.

I rolled over so that I would not have to breathe her perfume, which reached every wall of a room. William bought her a bottle every birthday, bringing it from a foreign country in a delicate, unusual box. When she had taken the perfume out, I would add the container to the line of perfume boxes along my dresser, because I loved the thought that they had been exposed to different air and that William had picked them out and bought them. Though I expressed none of these softer feelings to William, they had been shooting up.

"Leah," my mother said. "I just danced with him to show you how to relax, lighten up."

Then she got up, sat on the edge of the bed, sighed.

"I was thinking I might go down for a swim," she said, restless. "Feel like it?"

"No."

"Look at all the beauty." She pointed her toes in the direction of the window. Then she shuffled towards it, looked down. Next I heard her rummaging in her suitcase. When she tapped me, I opened my eyes and saw her in her burgundy bathing suit, a white robe over it. She hairsprayed her hair, then took something small out of the sidepouch of her suitcase, placed it in the pocket of her robe. She was going swimming even though William had never been able to get her in the water. A gold chain, a Christmas present from William, rested upon her tan.

"Night," she said.

She brushed out the door.

I rolled over to my side of the bed, where the sheets were still warm, the smell strong, sweet. I wrapped my portion of the blanket around me. I picked up the white phone, dialed my home number, and the rotary tone sounded like bees. The smell of perfume was on the phone, too. William answered, alarmed, defensive, his throat thick.

"It's Leah."

"Leah?"

"We're here."

"It's very late, Leah. Is something the matter?"

"No."

"Where is your mother?"

"Swimming."

"Say hello to her."

"I will."

"Goodbye, then."

"Bye."

William hung up first. I laid my head on my mother's pillow.

In the light, I looked at my hands, still young, long, and slender, as if they were living a life I had never known.

THE GIRL
WITHOUT ANYONE

I TRAVELLED by bus and train and then by subway to my first singing lesson with an opera singer, Lydia Patrin, who lived with her parents in a condominium because she had just returned from a divorce in Europe. The apartment smelled of spiced oil, comfort. I had expected someone prim, someone heavy, but Lydia wore jeans, a T-shirt, and running shoes. She was still towel-drying her curly hair, black and grey.

"We'll be here until I get my own place," Lydia said, smiling at me in a way that suggested I was conveying something private that I had not intended to. I did not intend to convey anything.

"That's fine," I said.

"Fine?"

"Mm-hmm," I said, to clarify.

"Think of another word. That's suitable. That's all right. Babies say *fine*."

"I meant it's okay."

She turned to the piano, pulled down a book of music. I shifted my weight from one hip to another, something I did against my will when I was nervous.

"Are you ill?" Lydia asked. "You're slouching."

"I'm fine."

"Fine," she said, resting the open music book against the piano. "You don't look it."

"I am."

"Well, let's hear you."

She turned so that she was facing the small apartment piano, placed her hands like claws on the keys. "A scale," she said.

The first time I tried to follow it, my voice cracked, exhausted from the singing I did at home, untrained singing, forced, loud.

She stopped, squinted at me. "Sing this time."

I took the deepest breath I could and followed the first five notes, but soon after this, my voice took on a mortifying desperate tone, a holler. When the scale was finished, I immediately composed myself.

"You have the voice of a four-year-old," Lydia said.

"I can practise."

"Lie down."

I knew I was a soul able to take chances, to risk pride, to feel my dignity disintegrate, all in order to become what I wanted, a singer with a drape of hair who sang for strangers in a bar. I lay down and Lydia kneeled over me,

a knee beside each of my hips. She placed her hands on
my diaphragm. "Breathe into my hands."

I did.

"Breathe again."

I took another breath. Then she had me stand and
breathe into her hands, one on my front and one on my
back. At last, I breathed correctly, into the right place.

"Follow me," Lydia said.

In a narrow room, she stood beside me in front of a
mirror. She made a nasal sound, then I had to make it.
Then I had to bend over and make the sound. I also had
to feel Lydia's diaphragm as she breathed, and it
expanded as firmly as a hot water bottle.

When the lesson was over, and I had shoved my feet
into heels—mature heels, borrowed from my mother—
I said clearly to Lydia, "I want to be famous."

"I'm not famous and I can blow you out of this room."

"I'll learn."

She led me to the dim front foyer, made larger by
mirrors; in the hallway leading to the bedrooms, I saw
something I had not seen on the way in, a framed photograph of Lydia in opera costume.

"I'm not promising anything," she said. She patted me
on the back, directed me to the door. "But we'll see
what we can do."

I glided all the way home.

My mother changed into her housecoat when she came
home from work, and her hair, usually tightly and
efficiently curled, lost its fluff. She had stopped going out

for walks; instead, she stared out the window, her hand straightening a fold in the sheers, water-stained at the bottom, and she had the breathing of someone waiting, the stretched neck. The air conditioning was kept too low, even in William's absence; he was the only one with a sense of economy, with any sense of how to keep money from dripping out of my mother's purse. The first time he had lived with us, she had stopped buying the most expensive nylons, the kind I loved that were packaged in an egg, and chose the cheapest. They bought dozens of hamburger patties at a time, bought a freezer to store milk. He often said that he had rescued her.

"I think I'd like to run for mayor," she said.

"Run for mayor?"

"Lots of people respect me around here." She let go of the drape. "Do you think I could?"

"Maybe."

She sat down, picked up her wineglass, sipped. "I know a woman whose husband ran for mayor. I'd make a good one. Of course, you don't think so."

"I'm tired."

"I'm not," she said. "Too much money, anyway."

She set down her glass because it was time for her nightly phone call to William, who had been staying in the Journey's Inn, living there while they took a rest from each other, a trial separation, one my mother blamed on Alec's disappearance. Apparently, William was now not only closed off, he wouldn't pay attention to her the way he had before. While she talked and listened to William, she watched the smoke of her cigarette curl up to the kitchen light.

Matthew came home after work to pick up beer, which he took to his girlfriend's house. He did this often, not even bothering to turn off the car.

"Home again?" he said.

"Practising."

"Why don't you come out?"

"Can't."

"Whatever toots your horn," he said. Then he rushed out.

In my room, all night long with the windows open, I practised my breathing, held my hands on my diaphragm, lay down and placed a book on it, breathed into it, watched it rise and drop.

Later, my mother went out to spend the night in William's hotel room. She would come home the next morning before lunch and sleep the rest of the afternoon.

I locked the doors after her, but the house never felt secure because there were too many windows.

In the late, night-time quiet, a thought unrolled slowly in my mind. I would tell my father what I wanted to be and he would applaud me.

My father didn't answer the telephone, probably because he was out with his wife, the one he had met in the laundry room of his apartment building. I finally replaced the receiver.

Trying to summon at least superficial courage, I hummed in the car on my way to meet a man who played guitar in a band and needed a singer. He lived in the rough suburbs of Scarborough, and my mother hadn't wanted me to drive there alone, but since I had got my licence, I had not let her drive me anywhere. Driving was one of the few times I was my own person, fully in control.

I parked the car in the parking lot of a donut shop, in which I would sit until it was the exact time to cross the street, enter the building, and ride the elevator to the eleventh floor. I wanted time to assess the situation, to prepare myself, to become a portion of the person I wanted to become. It meant shaking off every memory, every thought of myself, and imagining myself differently. To imagine myself differently, I would watch other girls and imitate what I perceived as their amazing, most graceful nonchalance. I knew about keeping my back straight, my eyes steady. I knew to chew gum or, even better, to suck something, something red that would colour my lips. And I knew it had something to do with making the other person feel less important, weak. The purpose of confidence was to throw other people off their feet. I wanted to be on the winning side of it.

Crossing the street, I had an atrocious taste in my mouth, stale, venomous, that rose from deep within. The balconies of the tall apartment building I was entering were cluttered with pots, furniture, blankets left to get wet in the rain.

The person who buzzed me up had a quick, furtive voice, almost angry. The hallway of his floor smelled of Indian food.

When the door opened, I saw no one, only the apartment covered in a plush peach carpet, a couch with plaid upholstery but no legs, a vase of pussy willow on the coffee table. Then a short man with curly black hair appeared from behind the door, rolling on a sock, the kind of man I would normally pity because he was too thin and his eyebrows were too heavy.

"I thought you were coming at one," he said, looking over my shoulder.

"We said two."

"I don't have a guitar," he said, leading me down a hall into his bedroom. "I had to get it restrung."

In his room, he pointed to a poster of a drummer in colourful, shining robes, tight pants, and long leather boots. "He said he would play drums for us." Then he pulled down his blind to stop the sun from coming in. He still hadn't looked me in the eye.

"You know him?"

"My sister's engaged to him," he said. "But he's in New York right now." He lay back on the bed so that his head touched the wall. "What would you wear on stage?" he said, still looking past me.

"I'd have to think about it," I said.

"Clothes are everything," he said. He put on black mirrored sunglasses too large for his face.

"I want to sing," I said. "I want people to notice that I can sing."

"I'm coming into twenty thousand," he said, getting up and putting on a yellow blazer with sleeves that were too short. "Car accident."

"An accident?" I said.

"Steel plate in my head. I'm waiting for the money before I can pick my guitar up."

"Do you want to hear me?"

"How are you going to sing without a guitar?"

"Just sing."

He got up and shut his door. Then he sat down and watched me, and I could tell by the position of his head that he was not looking at my face, but at my body, not with any pleasure that I could discern.

In the middle of the strange, cramped room, I took a deep breath. I had to prove that I could sing. I took another deep breath and I started singing, a song I'd memorized that I listened to and sang to when no one was home: "You've Got a Friend." I'd never sung it for anybody before, and now that I was, I realized how different it sounded, how without force. My voice was barely leaving my body, but I could not forget the person I was becoming, the person who would not experience shame. I pushed my voice harder, trying to breathe, but what I was doing was out of my control. My voice was simply rising out of me, curling up and down. And singing this song, this private song, made me feel more vulnerable than I would have felt without clothes. But I sang until the song ended; stopping early would have dissolved me.

"Ever thought about country?" he said.

"No," I said, my voice barely even. "And I wouldn't."

"Singers usually have what people want," he said.

"I'm going to sing," I said.

"You have nice eyes," he said. "You could do makeup commercials."

I opened the door of his bedroom, made my way to the apartment door. "I don't want to do makeup commercials."

At the door I saw two women sitting in the kitchen, both overweight, and one stared at me with shining, still eyes that held back laughter. I struggled to pull on my pumps; one of them had a crushed heel, and I had to pull it straight, slide my foot in while holding it straight. I'd had the shoes for too long and they made me furious.

"Maybe you'll get better," he said. He opened a series of locks.

"I'm going to," I said, with my professional, artificial determination.

That evening after dinner, when it was still light, my mother said, "William and I have just about sorted ourselves out. Make sure you lock the doors."

When she was gone, I called my father and he answered on the first ring, excited to hear it was me. I suggested we have ice cream, but he wanted to put flowers on my grandfather's grave. It was nearing the anniversary of his death. I offered to come along.

I held the gladioli like a tall toddler in the car all the way to the graveyard.

He carried the flowers to his father's grave. After laying them down carefully, he stood up, but we did not move; my father stared at the flowers, judging. I looked off into the trees at the highway, and then I was filled with the most wild hope again, hope that I could actually do whatever I wanted, that I could have a happy life.

"I'm going to be a singer," I said.

"A singer?"

I nodded. "I'm taking lessons."

"What makes you think you can be a singer?" he said.

"I just think I can."

"When have you ever sung?"

"I do now."

"I don't believe that," he said. "Have you told your mother this?"

"Yes."

"I'll tell you," he said. "You're not a little kid anymore. It's time to face reality."

"I am in reality."

"You're not special," he said. "I don't know who ever told you that you were." He shook his head in angry disbelief. "You have to be special to be a singer."

Walking back to the car, he gripped my arm. "I still love you, though," he said.

On the way home, he turned up the radio, tapping his hand on the wheel. "Listen to that," he said, glancing at me smiling, encouragingly. After a moment, he put his hand on my knee and told me gently that he wanted me to have a good, simple life, not to ask for too much, so I wouldn't be disappointed.

At the lights, a girl with a knapsack crossed. She was older than I was, but I had lived longer.

A few days later, I heard that William was packing up his things at the hotel and returning to my mother. A week before, I had called Loretta and she had invited me to a pool party. At Loretta's house, I cut around through the back.

Not seeing her, I crossed the crowded lawn to a picnic table and immediately opened a beer because I didn't want to be caught doing nothing. Loretta's sister was in the middle of the pool in a black inner tube, and two men who had played on my brother's baseball team were spinning her. The lawn and patio were filled with people Loretta had finished school with, people who had done the right thing and appeared not to recognize me.

Sitting across from me at the table were an Italian man and a girl with a neat blunt cut and no lipstick.

"Who do you know?" she said.

"Loretta."

"She throws a good party."

Then she stroked the Italian man's neck.

I carried my beer into the house, where I found Loretta. She was cutting a large chocolate cake.

"I'm here."

"Hey, man."

As we were carrying it out, she said, "Maybe you can sing later. What's-his-name brought his guitar."

"Maybe."

After eating the cake, I felt I belonged, and felt better. And sitting at the table was a good strategy because people always wanted to sit down, and this meant I would always have people around me. The two men on my brother's baseball team kept tricking each other out of spots. Although I had drunk one beer and a half, I avoided going to the bathroom so that I would not lose my place.

It was the Italian man who went to his car and brought back his guitar, a shining red wood one. I wondered if I could do it, sing.

He strummed with an assurance that, for a second, intimidated me.

"Feel like it?" he asked the girl with the blunt cut.

"Have a cold," she said, plugging her nose.

"Doesn't matter."

"Maybe."

"I could," I said, but he did not hear me. "I could."

"You sing?"

"Mm-hmm."

"You know this one?" He played the beginning of "Desperado," which I had practised because it had no high notes. I told him that I knew it. He began playing. I missed my cue and he had to start over. I tried to breathe. The next time, I came in on cue and concentrated on just staying with the music, music that warbled and turned in a way it had not when I had practised. My head tightened, the air around me blackened, narrowed. I felt myself struggling to be heard above the guitar.

When it was over, I looked around. I saw puzzled faces, faces registering a strange act. The Italian man said thank you in a way that was too polite and even, unimpressed. His girlfriend opened a beer for me, smiled. Accepting it, I shrank. One of the men on my brother's baseball team jumped into the pool with a slap, and after that, the attention was off me. Loretta's father said he was starting up the barbecue. He had been inside.

I had to be alone. I had to think about what I had done, how I had ruined everything. I was huge and foolish and red. I was doomed.

When I felt sure no one was looking, I got up. I went out the back gate.

Walking along, I needed something to tell myself before I got home, something to make myself feel better. I could not believe anymore that I was spectacular. I could not believe anymore that there were great things to come. I was a girl who had become a woman, and that was all. There was no ceremonial border to cross. It was a fact that had crept up on me, swallowed me, and simply transformed me into who I was, hardly different from who I had been all along.

I turned onto my street. From the end of it, I could see that the car was in the driveway, the car that my mother would now share with William.

The closer I got to the house, the more my heart pounded, the more a sick dread filled my throat. The grass was dark green, the grass I'd passed every day without ever noticing. And then I knew, but it was a feeling, not knowledge—a feeling that filled me with a cold steel pipe. I could not be held down. I would leave. I would leave ruthlessly and I would leave everyone and they could never have me back.

ALL THE MILES

A YEAR and a half after the accident, we had still not heard from Alec. We knew that he had sent a birthday card to his mother, one without a return address. Although my mother, William, and I sometimes went out in the car to look for him on the empty roads north of our town, we never saw him. In inviting me to come along, my mother would say, in a hushed, dark voice, "We're going out driving." The fact that I had made Alec leave left me with a peculiar feeling when I joined them. I knew, as my mother did, that William would never find him this way, but I enjoyed the time together in the car, a time of no disturbances.

Along the two-lane highways, it was too dark to see anything. At gas stations, William would stop, fill up the tank, then go in to pay. From the car window, I could see him pull out a picture and show it to the gas station attendant, someone who wouldn't really look at the picture, I knew, who would have only sex on his mind, the girlfriend waiting at home.

"No luck," he would say, slamming the door shut. An hour or so later, when I could hardly keep my eyes open, we would arrive home and a certain spell would be broken, the spell of the three of us silent in the car, locked together in the search. My mother and William would wear an air of failed accomplishment. Once, my mother told me that William, too, knew that he wouldn't find him by driving, but felt he had to do something to try because he believed that if he had been easier on Alec, Alec would never have been afraid to come home after wrecking the car. "It makes him feel better to look," she said.

One night, in the middle of February, I did see Alec at a bar close to the north end of our town, where houses thinned out and the streets grew wider. He came in with a friend at the end of the night, when Loretta and I were leaving after an evening of playing pool. I had not seen him since he had left and he seemed suddenly solid, with squarer shoulders. He looked like the other young men in the bar, confident, not the way he had looked before. I wanted to give him what he had always wanted, my devoted attention, to lavish it on him.

I made my way over to him, and I behaved the way I never behaved around anyone: brave and fluid.

"Where are you living?"

"In a trailer," he said. "With Kenneth."

"Thought you were living in Barrie," I said.

"No way."

"You going to talk to your dad?"

"Maybe," he said. "When I can start making some money."

"I want to go before the car freezes," Loretta said, pulling on her blue wool gloves.

"Have to go."

"Do you have to?" Alec said.

"Back next week, though."

"Bye."

"Bye."

The car, one of the last huddled in the parking lot, had not frozen.

"I thought we'd be stuck in there all night," Loretta said. "By the look on your face."

"What's that supposed to mean?"

Pulling out of the parking lot, she said, "Let me put it this way. You don't like your own brother, do you?"

"He's not my brother and no, I don't."

"Could have fooled me. He thinks you're going to make him a happy boy."

"No, he doesn't."

"Your family has always been weird, though," Loretta said. "That's all I can say."

"I don't like him," I said. "I was just happy to see him."

"Never happy to see him before."

"I am now."

The Tuesday after I had seen Alec, William asked me something he had never asked me before: to go out for a drive with him. The only other time we had gone searching without my mother, who was at cards tonight, was the first night Alec had left. I went because I felt this was another shift between William and me. He was learning to trust me, to see that I did not cause harm. We drove along roads that we may or may not have driven along before. We ate Pringles out of a can propped up between us. It did occur to me briefly to mention Alec, but deep down, I believed that the search was not the real mission of the drive. The real mission was to be enclosed in the car with William, someone I felt I hardly knew. That I should have told him was clear, and I thought I might tell him in the future, once I knew him and he knew me and we were solid. I also thought that the Alec I had found was not William's son, someone who was of use to him. The Alec I had found could be seen only by me, alone.

"Alec was always stubborn," he said. "Even when he was a baby, he always had to have his way. If he wanted a sucker, and you said, 'No, you'll wait until after dinner, my boy,' he'd find a way to get that sucker in his mouth. He had to have instant gratification."

I chewed a Pringle as quietly as I could. "He'll come back."

"And when he wants to disappear, he sure knows how to disappear."

"He'll come back."

"He can't face responsibility, that's what his problem is. That's always been his problem. Whenever he had a problem in math, he'd simply ignore it. He thought it would never bother him if he simply didn't look at it."

We came to a gas station. William slowed down, then sped up.

"Don't you want to show his picture?"

"I've shown it to them," he said. "They don't know where he is. Why should they?" He said this as if he had some new resolve, some unspeakable insight.

He turned back onto the road, and I was very close to telling William about the trailer that Alec was living in. As a matter of fact, I was very close to spilling everything.

The next weekend, I got ready to go to the bar by first securing the bathroom, as I always did. I had learned to perfect myself confidently, to apply the correct shade of eyeshadow, to improve my face with blush, to double the amount of mascara. The final touch was lipstick, red, like a parrot's wing. After this ritual, I took a spot in the living room, read the newspaper.

My mother was cooking dinner that I would not eat, since I did not eat on nights I went out. Once she had the potatoes on, she lit a cigarette at the dining room table.

"Going out with Loretta?" she said.

"Yes."

"To the bar again?"

"Yes."

"You can't go to the bar for the rest of your life, my dear."

And then the doorbell rang, the Saturday night door-bell, and I went out to get in Loretta's car and we drove up to the bar. On the ride there, I had an extra sting in my stomach, the sting of not knowing what I would do in the future, where I would go. Whenever I tried to sing, when no one was home, the sound that came out was flat, tremulous.

The bar was almost empty because there was ice on some of the roads. Loretta and I played haphazard pool, as we always did, for this was never our real reason for coming to the bar.

"I know why you came," Loretta said, hitting a red.

"To play pool."

Near the end of the night, Alec appeared.

He dropped his heavy black overcoat on the chair. "You came back," he said.

"I always come here."

"It's pretty boring," Alec said.

"We could go to the trailer."

"The trailer?"

"Just to see it."

"Dumping me," Loretta said. "I'm not surprised."

He stayed for a beer, during which Loretta questioned him about the trailer, asked if he planned to live there forever.

"Yeah," he said. "In a fucking trailer."

The way his voice rose reminded me of the Alec I had known, but I wanted not to remember. I wanted him to be someone who could not disappoint.

Later, after Loretta left, I drove with Alec along a two-lane highway. His small old Honda rattled and he drove too fast, not in daring way, but calmly, as if aggressiveness were second nature. The winds coming across the dead fields caused the doors to tremble. I thought of William and how I hadn't told him, and something became clear: Alec was a son and nothing else. He was not someone who I should keep to myself or should want something from.

"How far is it?"

"Not far," he said, his voice deeper than I remembered it, more measured and intelligent, polite.

"Where'd you get the car?"

"Got it for a hundred bucks from the guy at the candy floss place."

"Candy floss place?"

"Factory." He sped up to rev the engine, then slowed down. "Awesome engine. That's what the guy said."

"So, you sent your mom a card?"

"Yeah."

"Why don't you come back?"

"When I'm making fifty thousand a year, I will."

"Why?"

"That's all he cares about."

The trailer he pulled up to was frail and white, spotted at the bottom with rust. He pulled up to it too quickly, waving to a neighbour in a rose terry-cloth robe who was holding a mug of coffee at the open door of the other trailer.

He lived with a blond man, Kenneth, who wore army fatigues but was too soft and pale for them. He did not say hello to me. The small white fridge was covered with dark fingerprints, and I did not want to see the bathroom. Socks, underwear, white T-shirts, and jeans lay on his bed, the lower bunk.

"You didn't get that job, man," Kenneth said.

"Christ."

There was nowhere to sit but on the foam bench beside Kenneth, who was eating popcorn and watching a black and white musical. Alec ordered pizza, though it was unclear how he could pay for it. He turned the television up to a volume that turned my thoughts to fragments, made my skin raw. Kenneth, who had started drinking, kept smiling at Alec with sharp, amazed eyes. He smiled at me in this way, too. I had the sense that, to him, I was inanimate, a porcelain object.

"I'm thirsty," I said.

After opening the fridge and finding nothing, Alec went out and came back a moment later with a carton of juice.

"Where'd you get it?"

"Barbara went out. As always, too stupid to lock her door."

"Won't she notice it missing?"

"Stoner."

"Fuck you," Kenneth said.

I drank the juice guiltily as we watched a new program, one in which women in bathing suits fought each other, let out high-pitched, stagy barks. I allowed my wrist to lean carefully against the bone of Alec's wrist, casually, as if I were comfortable with touching him, as if it were easy and meant nothing, just a natural caring.

The pizza arrived and Alec made sure I had more than anyone.

"Good?" he said.

"Yup."

After we finished, headlights lit up the side window, a car door slammed; then the door of Barbara's trailer opened and shut. Kenneth retrieved the juice from the counter, shoved his feet into heavy black boots, and pushed out the door. The wind that entered in his brief departure filled the trailer with cold. I pulled my thin sweater sleeves over my hands and Alec brought me a comforter.

After a while, I said, "He's been over there a long time."

"That's his girlfriend."

He got up and turned out the lights, and when he sat back down and got under the comforter, his knee was touching mine in the casual, caring way that my wrist had been touching his.

"I don't like this show," I said.

He got up and switched channels, pausing on each station, stopping when I said so. I settled on a late night program, one that did not make me laugh and I did not care about. What I did care about was getting closer. I wanted to feel that he could not let go of me, that he lived for me.

"Looks like it's going to snow," I said.

"Yeah."

"Probably better if I stay."

"Where?"

"Here."

I untied my boots, carried the comforter over to the bed, pulled a pile of Alec's clothing to the floor. I lay down on my side next to the small, dark window, impossible to see out of. Alec watched television for a moment, then turned it off. I heard him kick his boots to the front door, pour himself a glass of water. He lay down beside me without changing his clothes, got himself underneath the comforter. Though he was not touching me, the warmth of his body spread to mine.

"I thought," Alec said.

"Thought what?"

"I thought you hated me."

"I did."

"And you don't now?"

"No," I said.

He touched my shoulder.

He didn't say anything. I could hear the heaviness of his breath, the concentration of it. He squeezed my shoulder and I allowed him to.

"You're beautiful," he said. "Kind."

He began to rub my shoulder. And then he breathed on the back of my neck, breathing that made my neck tingle, and the tingling felt good. It could have been coming from anyone. It felt gentle and exquisite, and I began to shiver. His breath grew closer, and he started rubbing my spine with his hand so that my back became hot. My muscles began to give in, and Alec began to become anyone, someone who was touching me.

I turned around. We hugged and touched. And while we did this, did everything that we were not supposed to, everything that was wrong, I began to feel that I was wonderful, the most wanted person alive, that I could not fail, that I never had.

The next Tuesday night, William wanted to drive again. As we put on our shoes and coats, I could tell William was excited, and that his excitement had less to do with driving and searching than it did with me. Earlier that night, he'd offered me a chocolate cookie, the kind he liked more than any other—a first. Also, he'd chosen a night when it would be only me and him.

"Maybe I'll even let you drive for a bit," he said. "I think you're a good driver." This was the highest compliment that William could pay, to entrust me to drive him, to entrust me with his safety.

But in the beginning, he drove. We glided and turned through town, past the train tracks, past the new sub-divisions, and then we cruised along the highway. I searched for a glimpse of a horse, a habit on distant roads. And as I peered out into the darkness, it occurred to me how incredible this was, to be driving along with William and to have him want to drive with me. I could be the child he had never had.

He pulled into a gas station, filled the tank. When he came back to the car, I said, "Can I drive?"

"I almost forgot."

We switched places and William directed me.

"What if you never find him?" I said, getting used to the steering.

"Well, then, I suppose that will be Alec's decision."

We drove into an area I recognized. I saw the plaza where the bar was. But then we were on dark roads again, the same turns and hills as other roads. As we barrelled along, though, the headlights lit up a yellow fence that I had seen before on the way to Alec's. A few

minutes later, I saw the two white trailers, small against
the sky, fragile, insufficient.

"Those are the people that really have it bad," William
said, nodding towards the trailers. And that was all he
said. No inquiries, no suspicions, because he had no idea.
Only I knew, only I could have brought William and
Alec together.

I could barely breathe in the car, so strong this time
was the urge to speak, to do the right thing. But the
farther away we drove, the calmer my breathing became.
I told myself it was too late. I told myself that Alec and
I had gone too far, that we could never live in the same
house again. But it was more than that. I would always
know something that William needed to know, that he
would need me for. And until Alec came back, I would
be the one he looked to, the one everyone looked to.

We had been driving for over an hour. Usually, after
this length of time, we drove home. But William wanted
me to keep driving, and not only did I feel a little easier
for having left the trailer behind, I felt that everything
had somehow become right; William and I could be a
team. Alec had lost his place.

It finally snowed heavily, but it was not a cheerful snow,
the kind you wanted to walk in. It fell out of a low,
heavy sky and it came with wind. The entire world
seemed threatening, agitated.

My mother was in the living room, drinking a liqueur.
William had wanted to stay a little later at the office, and

he would be home soon. Every so often, she looked out the window. At the dining room table, I flipped through the classifieds of the local paper.

"Anything in there?" my mother said.

"No."

"No?"

"No."

"You'll have to find something. I can't support you, if that's what you think."

"I know."

When William came home, my mother sprang up off the couch, went to the door to meet him. They got ready to go to a dance at the community centre, my mother in a black blouse and black pants, William in a new green suit. Since my mother had started to help William look for Alec, they'd been closer, were talking more. When my mother left, she said goodbye in a dispirited voice, as if I disappointed her, as if she no longer knew what to do with me.

When I was alone, I locked all the doors, sat down in the living room. After a few minutes, I tried my voice, tested its strength, but it was still flat, too soft. I would never be a singer.

Instead of sitting down, which I could never do, I put on my coat and my mittens and I went out in the new snow. As I walked along, I wondered if we would ever see Alec again. Then it occurred to me that he was privileged to be out of sight; disappearing was the right choice. It was not eccentric, but essential. When no one knew you, when no one wanted to know you, you had to fight your way out.

I had one possibility left. I could go back to school. I could become someone entirely different, a person with power, a person who went wherever she wanted, who locked the door to her own apartment.

I rounded the block and went back towards home, my boots squeaking in the snow. When I reached the house, it was grey, still, and quiet, the way it had always been.